First published in 2020

Dedication

Ann Chatterton for your unfailing friendship, encouragement and painstaking read through of my first and revised drafts.

And to my daughters Hanaa and Safia who have shown me the true meaning of the words Love and Relationship.

Foreword

by Mary Turner Thomson
Author of: The Bigamist: the true story of a husband's ultimate betrayal

Love is a strange thing. It can lift us to unimaginable heights or leave us in the depths of despair. It can make us lose our minds or make us feel whole again. It can help us feel in control or confuse us, leaving us wretched and dejected. Love can be fun and it can be dangerous - raising us to heights of passion and leaving us euphoric, obsessed, distracted and foolish. It can be addictive and destructive too. And all that can happen whether the love is reciprocated or not.

It is the basis of our society, the benchmark of success and the thing that most of us strive for. It is difficult to give an accurate definition of love, or have the last word in what each of us should do in its name, because it is a personal and intimate experience for us all.

Love can take many forms – from a parent, from a friend, from a child, from a lover and for yourself – but in my opinion true love is selfless and honest, heartfelt and pure. It is a rare commodity that should be treasured and nurtured with patience and understanding – and to accept love from another you have to be able to love yourself.

I only truly understood being in love when my first daughter was born – here was a child only moments old gazing at me with bemusement and trust. Suddenly I mattered and was entirely needed by another human being on a level I had not experienced before. Here was someone I would give my life for and whose happiness meant so much more than mine. She taught me so much – not least was the realisation that we teach our children by example. Through love our kids will copy what we do rather than what we say – their admiration for us makes us the perfect role model. It meant that I started to live my life by the advice I would have given her. For instance rather than staying in an unloving relationship with her father I decided it would be better to be single and happy – because I would never had advised her to stay in a relationship just to keep a father around for her child. Whatever I wanted for my daughter I had to do for myself so that I could show her the way. Not least that if I wanted her to love herself then I had to learn to do that as well. If I wanted her to be happy then I had to be happy too, giving me the excuse to look after myself as well. Love broke me but it also made me again, stronger, wiser, and more ready to face the world.

As my other two children were born that love for them, and for myself strengthened, and today I have one of the most loving and strong families on this good earth.

Ultimately all love ends and almost always with pain, either through change or through death – but mostly it is worth it for the moments, years or decades of joy that it brings. I was honoured to be asked to write the foreword to Love Bites. I was pulled into these windows of love and felt the characters' joy and heartache. It made me laugh and cry, it made me grateful for what I have and made me sob for what others have lost. I finished the last story with a sense of wonder at having experienced other lives. Liza has penned stories that are beautiful, frightening, surprising, mysterious, eye-opening, heart breaking and uplifting – just like love itself.

Contents

All Change and Mind the Gap

"I'm at an age when my back goes out more than I do."

Phylis Diller

All Change and Mind the Gap

Polly critically appraised her fifty-eight year old naked self, performed a twirl in front of the wall mirror and wondered aloud if she was really date ready.

The lumps, bumps and missing bits were a stark contrast to her twenty-eight year old self similarly twirling back in the day, sporting Janet Reger and luring her sexy American Clark Kent look-alike into bed.

"Those were the days," she sighed, not for the first time regretting giving up casual bonking for God when she turned thirty-one.

That decision, triggered by a car crash and embracing evangelical theology, had led her to husband number two, a musical stalwart of the church. But the righteous Christian pianist, who turned out to have some questionable fetishes, decided to play away with his organ and Polly, at thirty-three, found herself wandering yet again in the desert of singleness. The church demanded celibacy and Polly acquiesced.

Six years later and the fact she missed a good rogering, love and desire trumped the risk of hell and damnation. Polly married husband number three, ringing in the change by choosing a non-practising Muslim and moving to Canada. She wasn't sure if it was her destiny to be single that she had been fighting against or just that she was lousy at picking good men.

She believed good men did exist and she even knew a few, but they were either gay or married to others.

God, it seemed to Polly, was indifferent to her plight.

Polly gave herself another scan and self-scored a seven out of ten. No cellulite, visible waist, great skin and a comfortably voluptuous bum.

"What do you say, Cat?"

The black feline observing Polly from her favourite warm spot above the radiator on the window ledge in the bedroom blinked lazily.

"Typical you ask Cat and really, you score a seven?" interrupted Speech Bubble.

Polly shook herself, trying to ignore the inner voice of her nemesis.

"Yes, I'm a seven," she retorted aloud.

"Well if you think so Polly, who am I to argue?"

Polly eye rolled, feeling more fourteen than fifty eight.

Speech Bubble had emerged when Polly turned fifty, in the same way her imaginary friend did when she was five. A somewhat lonely only child, Polly's curiosity usually got her into trouble with her stern Scottish Presbyterian Grandmother. Speech Bubble was her voice, the critical voice of reason against a wayward and active imagination which either gave Polly pause for thought or something to battle against.

Polly and her neighbour had spent the previous evening bemoaning 'the change'. Why had nobody told them about menopause? Hot flushes were one thing, but memory loss and a daily hormonal roller coaster absolutely stank.

"It's as if all women, post period, are just not relevant," said Jay.

"Well, they're not going to make a profit from us until we're ready for adult nappies," giggled Polly.

Jay was also single and raising two daughters. Although Jay's ex, realizing he had lost a diamond due to carelessness, was at least still useful when Jay needed a job done.

"I saw your ex over again yesterday," Polly laughed.

Jay grinned. "Yep, apparently the new, younger, smarter, mail order bride is not as ..."

Jay circled her face with her fingers and ran her fingers dramatically over her breasts, emphasising her features and winked. Jay was gorgeous, a show stopper.

"But here's hoping I soon have a new fish to fry!" Jay handed Polly her phone and showed the profile she had created on a dating site.

"You should try too," urged Jay, scrolling through various pictures of men in interesting poses she had marked 'favourite'.

Polly shook her head. Had the opportunity for meeting the opposite sex really come to swiping right, thought Polly? Online hadn't even existed when she'd met her last husband. They'd used The Guardian and she'd been attracted by his voice message, sight unseen.

"At least think about it, Poll, what you got to lose?"

After several glasses of red, opening the door to accommodate their hot flushes and closing it again to accommodate Polly's chills due to thyroid, Polly downed her glass and blurted out: "I'm not sure if I want to actually meet a soul mate, fourth time lucky, or if I just need some good old mental health rumpy pumpy."

"Eewww," wailed the voice of Jay's teen daughter, entering the room at the wrong moment, clearly horrified at the thought of 'old people' engaging in sex.

Juggling her children, a full time job and hosting international students, Polly had been way too tired to even masturbate, let alone put on some glad rags in the hope of a real life 'Harry met Sally' moment since husband number three. But Jay was right. What did she have to lose? Polly decided to follow Jay's example, put celibacy on hiatus and dip her toe in the waters of love.

"Or should that be swamp," interrupted Speech Bubble unhelpfully, as Polly signed up to the site.

She chose the handle PBGD, short for Polly Brisbane Goes Dating. If nothing else it will be a good conversation starter, she thought. But Polly hadn't reckoned on PB, as in that good old North American favourite Peanut Butter, stimulating some unusual and creative fantasies from some of her would be suitors.

"And I bet he wouldn't offer to do the laundry after that sticky little scene," said Polly, as she and Jay laughed loudly at some of the more absurd suggestions.

Posting a picture was simple enough, the selfie hadn't extended her nose too much she thought, remembering her daughters' tips for looking slightly sideways and tilting her neck. She hadn't dared to ask one of them to take a snap. Too many questions and she was a terrible liar. But writing an honest, jaunty and hopefully appealing profile was like pulling teeth. It had taken Polly over a week to get right. She knew she was overly sticky about grammar but, as Speech Bubble pointed out, she was hardly writing an exam for English literature.

To her surprise, Polly received three messages within an hour of her post going live. Oh the power of the swipe, thought Polly, feeling mean as she dismissed two of the three instantly and sent a wink to someone called Reuben, aged 59.

A large man, Reuben's profile picture did not set her on fire, but the way he wrote about himself made her laugh and laughter, like sex, had also been missing in action since she and the children's father had separated.

A few days later, Polly and Reuben planned a date.

The beach walk and drinks led to dinner. Reuben was thoughtful, interested in listening to her chat about anything. He didn't mention peanut butter or ice hockey, the go-to subject of most Canadian males if her friends' husbands were anything to go by. His attention made her feel good about herself.

It was half way through the second date that something gave her pause for thought. Parked outside a cafe with his brother on speakerphone, Polly was taken aback to hear him confirm that he and "that lovely woman I told you about" would both be at his brother's house for dinner the following weekend.

When the call finished, Reuben beamed a broad smile at her. "You'll love my brother's house and family." Polly could feel the knot in her stomach growing tighter.

"Now isn't that thoughtful, Polly?" Speech Bubble interrupted her thoughts; the sarcasm was not lost on her.

"Actually, I'm away next weekend." Polly lied, feeling the crimson flush creep over her face from her neck upwards.

"Oh", a disappointed glance let her know he felt let down.

Polly pondered, wondering why she was feeling bad; she liked being described as a wonderful woman but there was something else niggling. Ah, choice, she realised; the assumption reminded her of her ex and his family. Her father-in-law crawling through the unlocked window with yet more curry, ignoring the note, 'Mother and Baby Sleeping, please do not disturb' she had posted on the front door.

Reuben's second glance reminded her of a dog who had displeased its owner. Sad wide eyes, his head nodding sagely. Appealing for an 'it's alright, boy' pat on the head.

"Sorry Polly. " He reached over and stroked her hand.

"It's okay, just check with me first in future if you want to do something together. I just like to be asked." Her voice was soft, not unkind, but it was clear.

If he'd had a tail, Polly imagined it wagging wildly. Poor lad, thought Polly. She was looking forward to getting home and sinking into a nice hot tub full of bubbles with a large glass of rioja, dating was exhausting!

Reuben redeemed himself and their next couple of dates were fun, no brother on speakerphone or surprise family get-togethers. Then it was his turn to be away, off to Montreal to visit family on the east side.

"I'll miss you, Polly" he had said sincerely as he'd bent in for a kiss. Polly ducked and Reuben's mouth hit the top of her head.

"Oops," she said, "just trying to stop Cat from getting out of the door." They both looked down. Cat, as if on cue, stood at the top of the stairs and let out a long meow, apparently nowhere near dangerously escaping. Reuben looked puzzled.

"Bye then," said Polly brightly, waving.

"You're a bloody difficult woman to please," said Speech Bubble snarkily as Polly closed the door with finality behind Reuben.

Why exactly had she ducked? Polly wondered.

A few days later, Reuben was on the phone telling her he had fresh bagels from Montreal for her and the girls and was on his way over to her house.

Polly, already in her PJ's, was confused. Had she said she wanted bagels? Were bagels a metaphor for, 'I want to come over and have you now'? Did he imagine covering her in cream cheese? Had he misread her duck for 'chase me' rather than what she realised later was indifference? Was his largeness down to a food fetish? Her imagination caused her to giggle. But it was past nine and Polly found his pressing urgency about bagels - about as welcome as mosquitos on a nudist beach. She felt the sad eyes from the other end of the line as she politely declined and clicked off, muttering, "Choices, Reuben, it's all about choices."

"Ha," said Speech Bubble, "and just how many choices do you think you have left, Polly Brisbane?" The moment was reminiscent of the day her eleven plus results had come in. Fail. The family were gathered in her grandmother's front room, reserved for guests and celebrations. "This is very disappointing, Polly," they had spoken in unison.

Polly narrowed her eyes, shook off the memory and dusted her hands together, suddenly fancying a bagel.

Encouraged by Jay and fearing if she hesitated she would not get back in the saddle, so to speak, Polly considered who she wanted to meet next. She sorted the incoming messages from the dating site into absolutely nots, possibles, warmly interested and ooh yes please, on the condition they had read a book or two, knew the basics of good manners, had good hygiene and didn't show up in a baseball cap. Her red lines didn't seem too demanding despite Speech Bubble's negative comments about her being picky.

"At your age Polly, surely you only expect crumbs, not the complete slice of cake."

She agreed to compromise on the baseball cap. But after a few dates with mismatched odd bods, including more than one sporting a torn shirt and a baseball cap, Polly reset her standards.

It was the beginning of fall when Polly agreed to meet Cal who's messages had made her laugh out loud on the dating site, and found herself headed out to a bar on the downtown waterfront. She knew the location well as the bar happened to be part of a hotel and restaurant she and the girls frequented. The date sounded promising but she felt a little sceptical as he had called off brunch at short notice earlier in the morning.

And there he was on the patio. He was lean, fair, good looking and definitely a ten.

She stepped out onto the top step of the patio next to him. Thank you God, Polly thought immediately. She offered up her daily habit of gratitude to the God she believed in, who now didn't fit into any box of church or mosque or formalised religion.

He drew her in for a hug, no ducking this time. He was warm from the sun and Polly found herself relaxing into him easily.

"Whoa there, Polly," urged Speech Bubble.

Cal handed her a glass of prosecco, "I hope that's okay," he said smiling, "or would you rather a cocktail?"

"I love Prosecco, especially this one. I take my wine tour guests there, but of course I can't drink it then."

"Of course, pretty Polly, you are the Gracious Grape. I thought your face was familiar. I wanted to talk to you at that downtown business mixer. I guess you don't remember me staring at you from across the room last summer, at The Belfry?"

Polly gulped, he was charm personified. How did she miss that, she wondered, and laughed her warm tinkling laugh, familiar to good friends and family. He held her gaze as she sipped her drink. Polly felt dizzy on his attention, she didn't need the prosecco.

"Another?" He smiled warmly

"Let me," Polly fumbled in her bag.

"Absolutely not," he insisted. "I let you down this morning, I have a lot to make up for."

He ordered a Prosecco for her and coffee for himself.

"I thought you might like to take a drive along Dallas Road, maybe see if we can spot some whales? It's such a lovely evening."

There had been a whale pod spotted very close to the shore line in the past couple of days. Polly closed her eyes and wrinkled up her toes. She wanted to do a happy dance and yell out to the other customers, "He likes whales!"

"Hhhmm," Speech Bubble put a warning shot through her excitement. "How old are you? Fifteen? Funny how you don't seem to mind plans being made for you this time around."

Polly was in the Ladies Toilet. She'd needed somewhere to calm herself.

"Totally differently done," she sniped back.

The other occupant combing her hair next to Polly looked concerned as the words slipped out aloud.

"Oops," said Polly nonchalantly, "Just having a few words with myself."

"Ah yes, I do that, especially when the other half is driving me mad."

Polly remembered what that felt like too.

With no whales in sight he suggested they stop for a bite at The Marina. He had something he wanted to tell her about himself, something he'd not been able to tell anyone for a long time.

Here it comes thought Polly, he's a lifer out on bail, he's a gambler, an addict of some kind. Why on earth had she just agreed to get into a virtual stranger's car?

"Okay," said Polly. Glad to be getting out of the car and free to make a run for it if necessary, despite the heels she had put on to make her legs look slimmer.

Their table, a booth overlooking the water, shimmering under a pink tinged sky was the perfect scene for a romcom, not the confessions of a serial killer, her imagination spiralling out of control. She put on her 'fake it till you make it' face.

"So," said Polly brightly turning to look at him, surprised to see his eyes were filled with tears.

"You're so beautiful Polly, you remind me of her, I'm sorry, that's partly why I wanted to meet you. But you're not. You're even kinder than I could have hoped for."

"Who exactly ...?" Polly asked cautiously. Was this his ruse to get her onside before he killed her, had he killed his ex?

"Too much CSI, Polly," interrupted Speech Bubble.

"My late wife. She died along with my daughter when she was driving to pick me up from the airport after a business trip. It was a horrible crash and I still feel so guilty - after all, if they hadn't been coming to pick me up, they would probably still be alive."

Polly was horrified. How could she have been so mean, so cruel to think such awful things about this poor dear man?

Polly's eyes also filled with tears. She put her hand over his and whispered, "I'm so sorry."

By the time he drove her home, Polly was enamoured with him in a way she hadn't believed was possible. He kissed her gently on the cheek and asked to see her the following evening, if she was free.

If she was free! Polly curled her toes in pleasure and had to restrain herself from a squeal.

"I have something to tell you," she said, "I'll be free after eight if that's ok?"

As she got ready for bed an email pinged into her mailbox. It was a thoughtful note from him, telling her he was counting the minutes until he picked her up the following evening.

He arrived with a bouquet of flowers for her and hot drinks for them both as they headed for a sunset vigil on the top of the highest lookout point, renamed Pkols. Polly told him about her cancer and the fact she had no left breast and they had to reduce her right breast so she had no feeling in that part of her body.

"It's one of the reasons I've been so reluctant to explore dating until now, that and the girls of course." she said.

He clearly cried easily, his cheeks were wet as he pulled her close to him, and told her that he knew what that was like because his late wife had also had breast cancer. That he would love her body tenderly, because he was already falling in love with her.

When he kissed her she believed him. How could she not? He suggested taking her to his beach house when she was ready, in her own time, to take things further. She could even bring along the girls if she was comfortable with that.

Polly went to bed that night content and happier than she felt she deserved. She didn't even need the radio to fall asleep.

It was the following morning that reality, as reality has a habit of doing, hit Polly like a brick through a window.

Waking from its do not disturb settings Polly's phone started pinging. There were three emails from someone she didn't know and five incoming calls from an unknown number. Polly was alarmed by the urgency of whoever was trying to get through.

The first email was a rant in which Polly was told, in no uncertain terms, just what sort of a woman she was, home wrecker and other choice superlatives that almost suggested she earned her living lying down. The second was a serious of questions and the third mentioned a man called Jim. There were no voice messages left. Who on earth was Jim pondered Polly? She pinged back a reply. 'Sorry, I think you have the wrong person. I don't know any Jim and I earn my living as a family support worker for women living with trauma, so you definitely have the wrong woman. I hope you find who you are looking for, but please delete me.'

"Well Polly," said speech bubble, "doesn't this sound like a juicy problem."

"It's too early for your snide remarks and, no, it sounds like a bloody awful mess. Poor Jim and whoever the women are."

Almost immediately another email pinged in with a picture of Cal, he of the dead ex-wife and daughter. 'This is Jim, my husband, were you out with him last night?'

Polly stood staring at her phone. There had to be a mistake. Cal was Jim? How could that be? Polly looked on the website of the business Cal said he owned. Yes, that was him, but according to the website his name was indeed Jim.

'Do you want to call me? I'm not cross with you,' stated the emailer, 'only we've been through this before, I thought he was done. I went through his phone and found the emails to you and your number once a friend tipped me off that she had seen his profile on a dating site."

Polly emailed. Call me.

It transpired that Ingrid was Cal, or rather, Jim's second wife. That there had never been a dead wife or daughter. He had married Ingrid a year after he was divorced from his very much still alive ex, five years ago. His daughter didn't speak to him.

"He's pathological and very convincing," said Polly.

"Yes, said Ingrid. I don't know what to do. We've already been through two rounds of couple's counselling."

"Dump him," said Polly unceremoniously. "He's a prick."

That night was time for the weekly walk, whine and wine with Jay. Any benefits from the walking were quickly undone by the wine tasting, the original concept for the get together with friends. Jay had no idea what had happened with Cal.

"Girls just wanna have fu ... u ... in." Jay's rendition of the Cindi Lauper hit could be heard over the vac she was using to clean up the inside of her car.

"I have most of my fun with you and my girls these days," said Polly as Jay, in full makeup and a glam top, pulled her body out of the car.

Jay grinned. "Poll, dya mind if we postpone tonight? I got a date with a guy who lives off the island. He's just here today. I should have called before I started to clean out the midden the girls have turned this car into."

That explained the make-up Polly thought, nodding her head.

"Of course not ...," her trailing voice betraying the disappointment she felt behind the smile.

"Have you checked him out, that he's really who he said he is especially if you're planning to go somewhere in your car?"

"Don't worry Poll doll, I'm from the North remember, we women are tough, we can take care of ourselves! You okay?"

Polly nodded, now was not the time to tell Jay what had happened and put a damper on her high spirits, but she couldn't help be worried for her friend. Northern toughie or not.

"Okay, but at least text me when you're back and let me know you're alright."

"Yes, Mum." Jay grinned wickedly, "If I come back that is."

Polly laughed. Cal was a one off, but the experience had knocked her confidence. The email she had sent him suggesting he get professional help, cc'd to his wife, had been satisfying in one regard but she questioned her own sense of radar, why she hadn't listened to herself that something was amiss, dismissing her thoughts as imagination. Well, at least he wasn't a serial killer, just a serial philanderer and liar. She decided to unpublish her profile and have a rethink. However fate, as fate sometimes does, had other ideas and Polly found herself out on three more dates without the help of the website.

An ex-colleague, she thought was divorced, but who also it turned out over dessert was still married chanced his luck over lunch, a former businessman who impressed by buying her coffee in the line-up at the local teas'n'beans showed his true colours by getting drunk on their first date, and finally a former journalist she met at a friend's exhibition who hit all the right notes but was allergic to cats. Priorities, Polly muttered as she looked at Cat snuggled up on her bed and turned down his invitation to a second dinner.

"Really Polly? Are you seriously planning to date Cat for the rest of your life?" questioned Speech Bubble.

Polly chuckled, "So that's that, Jay," Polly declared on the following walk, whine and wine night. Jay had not had much luck either and they consoled each other, opening another bottle of red and performing ABBA in Jay's living room like it was 1975.

"Really, you two need to grow up and get a life" said Jay's daughter, coming in to see what the hell was going on as Polly screamed uproariously, tripping over Jay's dog and falling in a heap on the couch.

"I'm on her side," chipped in Speech Bubble.

The two years since Polly explored dating had passed quickly and now here she was on the brink of an even bigger change, moving back to Blighty and settling in Scotland.

Polly hadn't actually been in Scotland since 1979. After her aunt died there was little to draw her to the natural beauty Scotland has to offer. But at sixty she yearned for her roots, the land of her maternal ancestors.

"You know the problems you have here will be the same over there?" asked Speech Bubble as Polly zipped up the one large suitcase she was taking with her.

Who knew that a sixty year old life could fit into a bag, Polly pondered. It wasn't quite true, she had rented a storage container for all the books, special memories and china that represented the 'mum years' in Canada, but the suitcase was all she needed to start over.

Who had she been before? She wondered. There was a definite gap between her former life and the one she was now leaving after twenty-one years as a mum, and before that a free spirit, a bit of a tart, a working professional, a divorcee, a religious what? A survivor? All the titles fitted, yet there was something missing, something not complete. It was what was inside of her that mattered, at least that's what she told her clients, women who had been through much worse than she had in their lives. Whose survival and tenacity were inspiring, made the work worthwhile.

Speech Bubble interrupted her thoughts in the same way that the stern unrelenting gaze of her grandmother had made her Grandfather falter. "Now there's eclecticism for you. You were never settled Polly, so dinnae think a return transatlantic journey is going to change anything about."

Polly clapped her hands over her ears, "Oh, do shut up!"

"Okay, hon, whatever you say," said Jay coming through the door to lift Polly's bag into her car.

"Not you, idiot," said Polly, laughing, suddenly unsure. The move had been a rash decision after all. "Am I doing the right thing?"

"Pol doll, whenever have you given a thought to the right thing, apart from for your girls? Go with your guts, your passion. This is your time. I'm going to miss you like heck though." Jay's eyes welled up as they struggled to put the heavy bag in the back of the car.

Polly landed in Glasgow, and stood for almost an hour gazing at the empty carousel containing a folded pram, a rucksack and a large battered box before she learned that her bag had had a change of mind and decided to stay in Calgary. The helpful lost bag person gave her a toothbrush, toothpaste, an oversized T shirt, a face cloth and a promise the bag would be delivered the following day. Was this a sign that her plans were not going to run quite as smoothly as she had hoped?

The excitement of the move and the reality that she was now on a different continent from her eldest daughter and in a different part of the UK to her youngest who was spending her gap year in London began to hit hard, but she was determined not to give in to the looming sense of 'what the hell have you done?'

"Mind over matter, Polly," she said pulling herself up by her bootstraps and making her way to the hostel she had booked into for the night. Within two weeks Polly was working, had moved into a flat and was excited to start her new life. Perhaps sixty is the new forty after all, thought Polly, impressed with her self-determination and drive.

Everyone whom Polly had a connection with in Scotland was long dead. Her Mother, who had wanted to come home after she died, was residing on a shelf in Polly's wardrobe in a pale blue box. Polly hoped she didn't mind that her current home was Falkirk rather than Stirling.

Making friends had always come easily to Polly, and Scotland, full of friendly folk, was easy to settle into and that led to her next dating experience aged sixty one and three quarters.

They met at a local film group and whilst he hadn't given her goose bumps or a tingling tummy, he had read several books and he wasn't wearing a baseball cap.

To say it was kindness that attracted Polly to have a fling with him is to damn with faint praise but, as Polly reflected later, perhaps it explained why her return to sex had turned out to be more Benny Hill than Fifty Shades.

Polly had not anticipated her acquiescence to seduction to be clumsy and rushed. She had imagined candles, wine of course and a strappy stylish silk number that would hide the bits she didn't want on display.

"Let's face it, even though I get away looking ten years younger with my clothes on, my bod is not the bod it once was." Polly said to herself in the mirror as she tried on her new dress. It was just Tesco's but she thought she rocked it.

Even Speech bubble seemed to approve the choice, her silence on the matter was unusual.

When he had tried to snatch a kiss previously, it hadn't created any tingles but then who feels sexy being kissed out of nowhere, standing by the cat litter? Polly was happy to give things a go if he chanced his luck again. But she knew she was second guessing herself as Speech Bubble popped up giving her a thumbs down.

"What are you, desperate now?" Speech Bubble was right, he really wasn't her type.

It was the middle of December, Polly could see it in his eyes when they met. Her new dress was apparently doing its thing. Was that why she bought it, she wondered, for him?

After a couple of drinks Polly suggested they go back to her flat to watch a Christmas movie. They were a tradition for her and the girls, something not on his usual list of Christmassy things to do and, as she found out later, there wasn't a lot of joy or tradition for him in the season.

Polly could plan Christmas for three hundred and sixty four days out of three hundred and sixty five. It wasn't perfect, magazine spread style, just lots of homemade gifts for everyone and that took a lot of planning.

Polly didn't have a television. She had furnished her flat minimally until she had the money to do it up. So they balanced her laptop on a pile of cushions in the middle of her bed - which was more comfortable than peering at it from the sofa, and watched 'Love Actually'.

Despite being of that generation where men make the first move, Polly was not ready as he lunged towards her. They bashed teeth. For a moment Polly remembered Reuben and 'the duck', and giggled. Not quite the response he had been hoping for by the look he gave her, but at least Cat was nowhere in sight.

"Ooops, sorry," mumbled Polly. "I just remembered something funny. It's nothing to do with you."

He looked tentative but clearly something was stirring, because he didn't give up; this time Polly was ready.

And here we are, thought Polly, a couple of sixty somethings having a consensual grapple in my bedroom, like awkward teenagers. Unfurnished and undecorated as it was, her bedroom could easily have qualified for a student bedsit.

"That needs to stay on," Polly mumbled as his fingers fumbled with the back of her bra, then, "Ouch," as he attempted to connect.

"Well that's that Christmas favourite ruined, " said Speech Bubble unhelpfully.

Polly soon discovered that twenty years without sex, ovarian surgery and menopause to boot, did not a happy vagina make. None of her doctors had raised the issue with her when they explained the side effects and negative consequences of cancer and removing her ovaries. After all, Polly thought, I was only forty something when it all happened. Surely they must have thought I might be having sex again one day but then, they were all middle aged men, so maybe not.

In good old fashioned style, his needs were greater than hers. Without preparation or foreplay she lay there, dry as a bone, watching him out of pretend closed eyes and, what she hoped, was a sexy pout as he exerted himself.

To add to Polly's excitement, his shoulder had been strapped up by his physio in bright orange plaster. An improvement on cat litter, but definitely not a turn on. The quest for change in her singledom was certainly less thrilling in reality than in her imagination.

"Mind the gap," said Polly to herself.

"Told you," said Speech Bubble.

"Could we stop?" Polly muttered feebly. "It's rather sore."

"Okay. Did you come?" He asked brightly.

Polly wanted to laugh, this time gut wrenching howls, but that would be rude and she didn't want to appear unkind.

"Stupid as well as impatient," noted Speech Bubble.

"Shut up, you're not helping," Polly muttered inwardly.

"No, it was a bit painful. Sorry," Polly smiled.

He smiled back. Silence filled the space like eternity.

Oh God. Awkward. She began to fiddle, plumping pillows and straightening the patchwork quilt she had made out of her daughter's toddler clothes. The irony of that was not lost on her as she observed the still prostate male lying next to her.

"Another fine mess you've landed yourself in, Polly," pointed out Speech Bubble.

"Unnecessary and harsh," she replied, cursing herself.

He reached out his arm, pulling her towards him for a post coital cuddle. Polly wanted to down a bottle of anything and have a warm bath. Instead she suggested they refresh their wine which sent him scrabbling under the bed for his glasses whilst she tripped over the remains of the Rioja.

"We're both a bit out of practice I think," he said

"You think?" said Speech Bubble ironically.

"Oh, it was fine, just hurt - maybe after twenty years women go back to being virgins. It's certainly the season," Polly said attempting humour and taking the blame whilst remembering how she used to have really great sex.

She wasn't about to let him know how she felt about her body not working the way it used to.

"Damn it, I used to be hot! I am ready to be so again," she mouthed into the bathroom mirror and resolved to consult Doctor Google on a remedy, if there was one to be had. After all, her mother had been on a date for her eightieth birthday in a hotel. It couldn't all be over. Surely?

Like a good girl, Polly trotted off to the pharmacy and chatted to the doctor over the phone, because face to face talking about this kind of stuff at her age was definitely out of her comfort zone.

It was a week later when they tried again. He wondered if she wanted to be on top this time. But, remembering a friend's advice from years ago, about women over forty and facial gravity, Polly declined.

Polly lay back and thought of England, Canada, LA and other places she had lived. The plaster strapping was gone, but she was decidedly not feeling tingly.

Trying to relax and go with the flow she was unnerved as he asked, "Are you OK? I can go on forever."

Whoever invented Viagra needed shooting, she thought.

"Lucky you," said Speech Bubble as Polly squirmed.

"Sorry, it's still a bit painful. I'll need to stop," she said, with a sigh of relief as he obliged without protest.

A few days later Polly's youngest quit her au pair post in London and moved back home to save for uni. His son still lived at home so there was nowhere for the attempted romp to continue but, as he agreed, intimacy did not require physical closeness, although of course if he wasn't so daft he could have booked a room from time to time. The pessaries were doing the trick and Polly was liking the fact that a tingle was beginning to emerge.

"You go girl," said Speech Bubble!

Polly grimaced, it was rather disconcerting to have her nemesis cheering her on sexually.

Six months later the story that boys of fourteen tell their girlfriends when they have an eye on another hottie - it's not you, it's me - fell out of his mouth, rather the way a turd squishes out of one's arse after a night on the town after curry with chips. Plop. Her fantasy of how things might turn out if they tried again burst. Dumped without a do-over!

Thankfully Speech Bubble took over. If Polly had said what was really on her mind ... let's just say people have been arrested for less.

She typed a polite email and considered his generous offer to be 'friends'.

"Ha ha, that old chestnut," said Speech Bubble. "Friends is where he does what he likes, until one rainy Sunday when he tells you he's made a horrible mistake. You are after all the woman of his dreams. Hey presto, then the hamster wheel spins again, and he realises he needs another break, more time to be alone. Poor wee thing."

'Thanks, but no thanks,' Polly typed, as she added an emoji to let him know she was sad.

Speech Bubble smiled and nodded, "Smart choice."

Polly poured herself a large glass of red wine and toasted herself. "It's just the beginning and who knows where the next few years will take me," she said aloud to Cat, embracing optimism despite the uncertainty of what lay ahead.

Speech Bubble nodded, for once her voice was gentle, not sarcastic or critical.

"Just mind the gap Polly."

Polly looked up, realising that the choices she made, the changes she chose did indeed lead to gaps, gaps in her sexuality, gaps of knowing who she was other than a mother, and now the biggest change of all, ageing.

She planned to be around until her daughters were settled, so at least another twenty five years. Almost enough time for a silver wedding anniversary, she thought, as she browsed through a Scottish dating app, closing it again, without registering. I've been dating since I was fourteen, had three attempts at marriage and several lovers. Do I really need to go there again she wondered?

And, as if the angel of the algorithm had been listening to her thoughts an ad for a famous chain of sex shops popped up. Polly clicked the link, and flicked through what was on offer. She giggled at the image of a woman pleasuring herself, well there was always a handy courgette or two in the kitchen.

"Polly Brisbane, you are a wanton and naughty child, always were and always will be." And she was back the critical voice of Speech Bubble, offended by harmless fantasy yet protective of Polly's naivety.

"Yes", agreed Polly. "I am, but I am also lots of other really positive things and I don't need a man in my life to make me feel better about myself. I don't need a woman either, just in case you were wondering, but I do want, genuinely want pleasure, and I think I have found how to manage that."

"With courgettes?"

Polly shook her head smiling. The clarity of shock and disgust in Speech Bubbles voice reminiscent of her grandmother's views on sexuality and pleasure. Her grandmother had not even undressed in front of her grandfather, possibly had not even see herself naked since she was first married. It was a miracle her mother and her uncle were born. Polly remembered her grandmother changing under the big floor-length pink white or blue winceyette and cotton nightdresses that resembled tents. Presbyterianism had a lot to answer for.

Polly put her hands behind her head and swivelled her legs up to recline on the couch, Cat purred and jumped on her belly.

"You and me then Cat," said Polly stroking the purring feline she had spent a small fortune flying from Canada to Scotland via two planes, a bus, three taxis a ferry and three trains. She was determined Cat was not flying cargo.

A feeling of contentment that had been absent filled her like a deep cleansing breath.

"Thank you," she uttered under her breath. Not needing to please anyone in particular, not the God of do and don'ts, or the historical baggage she had trundled around for years. It was time to let it all go. Begin over, change the self-doubt, critical voice and not worry about the gap as she leapt into the unknown, embracing a new found freedom.

A Moment in Time

"I have reached an age where if someone tells me to wear socks, I don't have to."

Albert Einstein

A Moment in Time

It's a silly thing to do really thought Pam to herself as she prepared the old camper van, but she couldn't back out now, especially after putting her foot down so strongly against her daughter's protests and already booking two weeks holiday off work. It was a matter of principle. It was true that The Westfalia had seen better days but the mechanic who had given the van a recent overhaul assured Pam it was still fit for purpose and would easily make the five hundred mile return journey. Betsy, as she and Robert had initially christened the bright yellow brand new camper, which they had bought to celebrate their tenth wedding anniversary in 1978. They had taken them and their children all over Scotland, Ireland, England, France, Germany and the Netherlands in it over the years. They had slept in her, made love in her, fought in her and, if he had had his way, Robert would have died in her. But his illness had progressed more quickly than the doctors had predicted and his life ended in a hospital bed, the last place on earth he wanted to die. That was five years ago, two days before their thirty second wedding anniversary.

Pam's heart sank as she saw her daughter Veronica's car pulling up outside the cottage.

"Grandma, grandma," the sight of her five year old granddaughter, Poppy, running past the lupins in full bloom soon extinguished her anxiety. Veronica would not have brought the children if she had come for another row.

"Hello Poppy, what a lovely surprise and how lucky I made some biscuits yesterday." Pam had baked shortbread, Robert's favourite, for her journey to have with the endless flasks of tea she would need to keep her going on the drive south.

Pam didn't like driving, for the most part when they had travelled, she had navigated whilst Robert drove. Some of the mountain roads had been pretty hairy. Her idea of speed was a steady forty five, meaning the journey would take over ten hours instead of the average five and a half.

"Grandma has shortbread," Poppy called to her younger brother Jonathan, as he barrelled in from behind on the new bicycle with training wheels he had insisted on bringing.

"This is a surprise," Pam greeted her daughter with a hug.

"Yes, well, I'm sorry about the phone call. I've been told off by everyone for what I said."

"Everyone, meaning your husband and your brother?" queried Pam.

"Yes, and even my sister in law, damn it." Her tone was playful, but Pam wondered if that's how she was really feeling. Veronica was hard to read sometimes.

Pam laughed, "Part of the downside of being from a close family who cares, Veronica, wouldn't you rather that, than.... - "her voice trailed off, she had been about to say being alone, but she couldn't face the word. "Come on, I'm so glad you came, I'll make some tea. Juice for the kids okay? I'm pretty low on milk, apart from powdered."

"Do you have anything a bit stronger - for me, not the kids," Veronica giggled. "If it's okay we thought we'd stay up overnight and give you a proper send-off tomorrow." Veronica looked uncertain, after the row perhaps it was too much to ask the night before her mother left to hug a tree.

"Tea for me, Gin and Tonic for you and yes, you staying would be lovely, so long as you don't mind sorting out the bedding and such, I've still got lots to do getting Betsy ready."

The last time Betsy had had an outing was when Pam had taken Poppy and Jonathan for a weekend campout whilst her daughter and husband went for a much needed romantic getaway. A year ago, Pam had been worried her daughter's marriage would not survive, but they seem to have turned a corner. Pam scraped the sticky remnants of goodness knows what the children had left there from under the fold out table. Cleaning thoroughly had never been her strongest gift. Robert had always laughed about the piles of clutter stuffed hurriedly into cupboards when they had guests over, especially his parents. His mother was the queen of neat and clean.

"Are you really sure about this Mum?" Veronica minded her tone as she asked the question of her independently minded mother. They were making a pasta bake for dinner together. Veronica's concern about her mother's planned trip was how the row on the telephone had started and she didn't want to end up there again, but she couldn't help worrying.

"Am I sure that I have a mind of my own, that at fifty eight I am capable of knowing and understanding what I am doing? Please don't patronise me, Veronica."

And that was that, the line was drawn. Her mother had always been good at boundaries, had to be in her line of work as a social worker in youth justice.

"Enough said, of course you know what you are doing," Veronica demurred, pouring them both a large glass of wine.

It was two weeks since Pam had read about the protest gathering around the removal of five ancient oaks in Dulwich in the Sunday Times. Since then the mounting local pressure had become bigger, turning into a national protest campaign to save the trees. They were being removed as part of a new ring road system to accommodate some much needed affordable housing. Pam was torn, she knew the local families would need housing, she had advocated for similar housing often enough on her own patch in the Pennines at local council meetings, which had not made her popular with the Nimbys. But, those magnificent trees in Dulwich pulled on her heart strings. One of them was rumoured to have been the inspiration for The Magic Faraway Tree, the bedtime favourite of both her brood and the go to book she read and bought for the children in her care. There was something about those stories, the different lands on clouds which captured the imagination, and in the case of some of the children she had to place in foster care or adoption, hope of a better life to come. Pam held the writers' ability to communicate with young people through their imagination in esteem, but concurred with her colleagues some of Blyton's other works did not fit the changing winds and recognition of a more progressive and inclusive environment. The world was complex, Pam ruminated; she was a lateral thinker, never quite managing to stay inside the lines.

"Where are you going, Grandma?" asked Poppy the following morning as the final bag was stowed in Betsy.

"I am going to save a tree, perhaps a very magical tree." Pam smiled down at Poppy whose freckled face and button nose was almost the spitting image of Veronica's when she was five and not so very different from Pam's as a child. Jonathan took more after his father Michael.

"Are you going to bring the tree home to your garden, Grandma? Can I come with you?"

Pam smiled and hugged her granddaughter. If she wasn't careful she would spend the morning caught up in the delightful world of Poppy and her never-ending questions, rather than getting on the road and making it to Oxford and the bed and breakfast she had booked into for the night. There was also a bookshop there, she and Robert had loved. She would be spending enough nights in Betsy once she got to Dulwich and she liked her creature comforts if truth be told.

As she waved them goodbye, Pam realised she had told Poppy she was saving a tree, not trees. Should she have told Veronica the reason the destruction of the copse was so important to her was because it was there that Robert had proposed? But Veronica, unlike Pam, was a black and white thinker, she didn't have the same attachment to places or things that Pam did.

1965 was almost another world, a cloud where the beat of pop music and a culture of optimism and hedonism was sweeping London like a tsunami, dismantling old ideas for new. In some ways, it had all been rather frightening for the nineteen year old Pam who came from a god fearing Baptist family in a northern village. But meeting Robert changed that and he swept her off her feet with his brilliant satire and radical ideas, taking her to clubs, introducing her to books and music that challenged her narrow lens and how she perceived the world around her. They went to concerts at Longleat and the Isle of Wight, protested in Trafalgar Square and, when Pam turned twenty-one, he asked her to marry him, going down on one knee under a five hundred year old oak tree in Dulwich.

Pam had not expected such a traditional proposal from someone as non-traditional and modern as Robert. It was a glorious June day, they walked for hours hand in hand, before spreading out the tartan rug under the shade of the old oak. He was celebrating his finals and Pam had arranged a picnic with champagne and as many of his favourite foods as she could afford on her meagre student allowance to mark the occasion. The copse was one of their favourite places; it reminded them both of their rural childhoods, his in Wiltshire and hers in the Pennines. He stood up to carve a heart with both their initials into the trunk.

"Do you care for me, Pam?" he had asked.

"Care for you? Of course. More than care, I love you, Robert!"

It was then that he dropped onto one knee in front of her and asked her to marry him.

"Yes please," she had said without hesitation or worrying what her parents would think about her marrying a poet with long hair who didn't believe in their God. Robert embraced the world with such love and generosity, more than she had ever seen or heard being preached in the Baptist church. The church which seemed more intent on making the congregation feel badly about themselves and their committed sins than about loving their neighbours and feeding the poor. Pam knew, in her parents' eyes, her engagement would go down as one of her sins, but she didn't care. She loved Robert more than life itself.

"Will this do for now?" he said as he wrapped the stem of a buttercup around her finger and carefully pulled through another to crown it, as though it were a huge yellow gemstone.

"It's the most beautiful ring in the world" she said as she kissed him. They captured the image on his Kodak Instamatic and the tiny monochromatic print they had framed still hung in her bedroom.

The traffic on the motorway was not as bad as Pam had thought it would be as she chugged along in the slow lane, but the weather was not with her. Driving in the rain made the journey seem more hazardous somehow. Veronica had made her a tape for the long drive with her favourite songs, a mixture of pop, ballads, classics and jazz. The current song, Judy Collins "Both Sides Now" seemed apt as she missed the turn off she needed, adding another ten miles to her journey and making her way back along the other side of the motorway. "Damn it" she said aloud, as spilled tea and crumbled shortbread congealed together on her jumper.

It was gone ten at night when Pam finally arrived in the tree lined street she had selected to park Betsy. She had spent longer in Oxford than she meant to and was feeling frazzled as she struggled to park in the only space left.

In a flat overlooking the street Inspector Geoffrey Knowles, was reviewing the case notes about the increasing numbers of people descending on his patch in South London. He was one of the younger inspectors, not yet forty. But his wife's death had aged him and his attitude.

"Blooming tree huggers," he mumbled as he finished his unsatisfactory evening meal of scrambled eggs and burned crusts. He had forgotten to shop and by the time he arrived home at the flat he couldn't face going out again. It had been, in his own words, "a bugger of a day."

"Tuna treat for you tonight, Twinx, not that you'll mind." He said to the cat, mewing and nuzzling his legs. His wife had rescued the tabby female from a shelter, three weeks before she was run down and killed. Geoffrey hadn't been a cat person, preferring the more regulated and dependent approach of dogs. But the cat had grown on him and with his irregular hours a dog was out of the question. After Daniella's death, Maggie had become a comfort as she settled down beside him at the end of each day.

Geoffrey decided to make an early start, there was nothing for breakfast and he'd cut himself shaving. The day was not shaping up well and it was only seven thirty am.

"What the devil?" Geoffrey cursed as he tried to manoeuvre his car from the narrow parking spot reserved for residents. The yellow Westfalia was parked legally but badly on the street outside the entrance and he had to stretch his neck to see whether it was safe to pull out. The dishevelled woman getting out of the van looked as though she had slept there overnight.

Geoffrey pulled over in front of the van.

"What the hell do you think you're doing?" he yelled as he strode towards the Westfalia.

"Sorry, are you talking to me?" said Pam undeterred by the gruff voice, she was used to dealing with angry men. "Big voice, small dick" she muttered to herself before looking up and flashing a smile.

"Yes, I am talking to you. This is a residential area. You can't sleep here and the way you have parked, you're too far out from the pavement and facing the wrong way." He knew the last point did not apply, although he wished it did, like in Canada where the cars had to park on the side of the road, facing the direction in which they had been driving. Not higgledy piggledy with bumpers facing bumpers instead of boots. But his petition to the Council to make that a local bylaw had got him nowhere.

"I know this is a residential area, and thank you I am well aware of the bylaws in regard to sleeping and I haven't broken them. No I am not too far out from the kerb, although I agree I could have parked a little more snugly."

Geoffrey was taken aback. He had not anticipated the diminutive woman to be quite so feisty. He knew he was in the wrong but the parking had got his goat. It was a badly parked car that had contributed to Daniella's death, hence his petition to make changes.

"Are you planning to stay here then? Moved into the neighbourhood in that thing?" Geoffrey knew he should have dropped it, moved on, got on with his day, but there was something infuriating about her, not helped by his empty stomach which suddenly erupted and rumbled loudly.

"Ah, perhaps you are hangry?" noted Pam in response. "My son doesn't do well without breakfast either. Would you care for some toast?"

Geoffrey couldn't believe the cheek of her. Hangry indeed, what a ridiculous expression although he knew he had let himself down, allowed the emotion of the moment and the perpetual grief to take over his usually composed and professional persona. He was about to decline when he noticed a placard with "Save the Trees" in bright green poster paint, decorated with brown buttons like acorns in the outline of the drawing of an oak tree. The banner was propped to dry beside the open door.

"You're here to protest then?"

"Indeed," said Pam, handing him a mug of hot liquid. "Sugar, milk?"

He felt his hackles deflating like an old balloon as he accepted the tea, observing her already making the proffered toast.

"Come in and sit" she patted the built-in bench seat.

Geoffrey was over six feet tall, he felt like a giant, entering into her domain. He had never seen the inside of a Westfalia at such close quarters before and was impressed by the design, how much could fit into a tiny space.

"So what was up with you this morning, just me and Betsy, or something else on your mind?"

She seemed to have read him like a book, from her observation that hunger had contributed to his anger, to what had kicked him off. The trigger point as the grief counsellor referred to it. "When nothing makes sense and you are overwhelmed by feelings of anger, sadness or both." Geoffrey recalled the words as clearly as if they had just been spoken.

"What makes you think that?" He was curious about what she had observed. He had been back at work for six months following the breakdown. Were his emotional wounds still so obvious?

"Well for one thing, most young men don't see women of my age, let alone bother with them."

"Young?" Geoffrey laughed. "I'm not that young."

"Well, when you are my age, everyone seems young."

"I'm thirty eight, you? Or is that impolite?"

"Very, but I have nothing to be ashamed of, fifty eight." she retorted almost playfully. "I have a daughter two years younger than you and son of thirty four." As the words came out, she wasn't sure why she had felt the need to tell him the ages of her children, to make him feel more comfortable around her perhaps?

He was surprised by her age, she was lithe, her long highlighted hair suited her complexion which was unlined and lightly freckled. He realised the highlights were in fact streaks of silver, not dye as he had first thought.

"Thanks for the tea and toast. You were right, I did need a little something, but work calls. I should warn you, if you are heading to the protest that there will be quite the police presence there today."

"Oh I'm sure they will be there in droves. Tree protestors are such a threat," she said, waving her arm flippantly. "Thanks for stopping by. If you live around here, you may have to put up with Betsy being parked until I go home, but I'll pull her in closer to the kerb."

He wondered why she hadn't asked him about why he had mentioned the police, perhaps she had guessed. Most people did, and then they backed off, didn't tend to invite him in for tea and toast. Most of his friends were in the police and Daniella had been too. That was how they met.

Pam watched him navigate his way along the road and turn towards the park. "Hmm, I was right," she said to herself. In her job, she had met enough policemen to know one when she met one. Most of them were like her, wanting to make the world a better place but there were one or two whom she had disliked intensely and took to task for not doing their job. Her size and stature hid the full force of her personality when she was riled. When she was crossed or saw injustice, Pam tended not to keep her feelings and opinions to herself. Robert had shown her that side of herself, helped her view things critically, and know when to make a stand.

Pam manoeuvred Betsy closer to the kerb and now the car that had taken up two spaces the night before was gone, she moved further away from the entrance to the block of flats the policeman had turned out from. She wondered if he lived there, or if he had been on official business. The fresh shaving cut on his cheek suggested the former. She realised they had not exchanged names, she wondered what he was called and his rank, unaware she would soon find out.

Making her way along the tree lined avenue towards the park, memories of walks with Robert haunted her. "I wish you were still here, my darling," she uttered the thought looking up at the passing clouds dotted about the blue sky. A small speckled bird started chirping as she passed under a spectacular birch tree in full leaf. "You would have known that bird, wouldn't you? How much you knew and cared about nature."

It was not unusual for Pam to have these conversations with her dead husband, they were raw and comforting at the same time. She fondled the tiny silver locket around her neck which contained two pictures. Along with her engagement and wedding ring, Pam hadn't taken the locket off since his death. Before that, it had lain in her jewellery box untouched for years. Robert gave her the locket just after Ian was born, and put a picture of each of the children which he had taken, inside. Pam removed the pictures and replaced them with a tiny black and white headshot of Robert when he was young and a colour one of him on his fiftieth birthday.

When she turned the corner, Pam was surprised by the length of the line of young and old protestors holding placards outside the park gates. It seemed the police had blocked access to the copse itself and there were angry voices shouting protests about the right to protest. A chant soon started up with the crowd responding "let us in, save the trees."

An organiser was handing out green fabric sashes and white t-shirts in return for a donation to the cause. Pam fished out two one pound coins from her bum bag for a sash. The press were there, cameras clicking and flashing at the protestors in what seemed like random habitual clicks. Pam wondered where all those photographs would end up, on some poor junior editor's computer perhaps? A reporter with a microphone was trying to elicit statements from the crowd, pulling individuals prepared to appear on camera to one side. Pam avoided eye contact with her, she had promised Veronica and Ian she would not go too public, they had already admonished her for her post on 'My Space'. There was also work to consider, and how her role as a protestor might be perceived by the Council for whom she worked.

It was mid-morning when there was a sudden surge in the crowd and Pam felt herself being swept along. As the line gathered momentum, she realised the crowd was determined to cross the barrier and get into the park. Some of the younger ones broke rank from the line and started climbing the railings. There was jostling and pushing from the back and suddenly the line deteriorated into a mob who stormed the barriers. Protestors took the chance to run unimpeded towards the copse. Pam decided it was safe to make a dash for it too and joined a small bevy of mostly female protestors close to a large tree on the edge of the copse. A young man was walking round the group and Pam realised she and the others were being roped in and chained to the tree. Pam could have stepped out. Indeed there was a moment when she thought about that option and decided against it. "In for a penny, Robert would have said," and she agreed, adding her voice to the chant. "We will not be removed." Her adrenaline was pumping around her and Pam felt more alive than she had since Robert had died. He's cheering me on she thought as she allowed her voice to become louder and louder. Her only regret was not thinking about going to the loo or wearing adult nappies before she found herself tangled up in the centre of the protest, not that she had intended to get chained to a tree. After almost an hour of holding herself in, Pam was desperate.

"I need to pee badly," Pam said to the younger woman standing next to her.

"Oh that's easy, we thought of that, you can just unclip from here and slip under the rope, but make sure you go to the back of our circle and deeper into the copse. The copse is surrounded and secured on all sides so you're safe in the middle.

"Amazing" said Pam, reflecting back to the chaos of the anti-Vietnam marches in Trafalgar Square. But in those days, her bladder had not been such an issue."

"Yes sir," the young constable responded to instructions from Inspector Knowles. The Inspector had just had both ears blasted. First from his superiors wanting the protest cleaned up and then by the Council whose delayed contract with the developers was costing a fortune.

Knowles felt the way forward was to let the protest take its course, let the protestors spend a couple of nights out in the open. It was bound to rain. They'd soon get tired and when the bulk of the protesters left they could deal with the stragglers. He had instinctively known that closing the park would lead to more conflict which it had and now he had to figure out how the careful and surprisingly well planned operation to close off the copse could be dismantled, without anyone getting hurt. Geoffrey was ten when the Brixton riots had taken place and his father, a reporter, was seriously injured. The rights and wrongs of how the protest was handled was not lost on him as he saw his father battle with the ensuing PTSD that had led to a life of alcoholism and an early grave. He didn't want to get this wrong. But he didn't have the last say and early on Monday morning the protestors were overcome by using force, including tear gas and batons.

It was late Tuesday evening when Geoffrey realised the Westfalia had been parked outside his flat since Friday, and there had been no signs of its owner since their initial conversation. The forced removal of the protestors early Monday morning had created a media storm and a court injunction compelled the police and Council to back down. Protestors were once again in the park. Maybe that's where she was. Whatever had happened she had made her own decision to participate, so the responsibility for her welfare was hers, not his. She appeared to be quite capable of looking after herself. Twinx mewed up at him. "Really?" she seemed to say. He looked at his watch, it was gone ten. Twinx mewed again. "Alright, alright, I'll go down, see if she's back at least."

He was in time to see her pulling up in a taxi as he turned out of the flat. She was limping and her arm was bandaged in a sling. She looked small and vulnerable as she unlocked the side door to the van.

"Are you alright?" he called out, not wanting to get too close and scare her.

"No. Thanks to your lot," she retorted.

"Ah, you knew I was a policeman then?"

She nodded.

"Can I get you anything?" He surprised himself by the question, what on earth was he thinking. She clearly thought that too, the way her eyes flashed back at the question in a non-verbal response of what on earth?

"Thanks, but no thanks. I'll be quite fine with some more Panadol and a large whisky. Goodnight." She pulled the door closed and he heard the lock click before he could reply, wish her a goodnight too.

"Well that told me, Twinx," he said to the cat who was already in a circle, tail over the nose, on her side of the bed next to the pillow.

Geoffrey had a sleepless night. He couldn't stop worrying about that damn woman in the van outside and at the same time all the good work he had put in with the counsellor seemed to be unravelling. Daniella's death had been thoroughly investigated as a traffic accident, but he'd always had a twinge of a conspiracy theory about the driver of the car. A niggle that was growing arms and legs again. After all, the wretch was known to the police. And then there was their daughter Nicola, still living with her aunt and not wanting to come home. What a mess. The thoughts turned over and over in his mind like a tumble dryer stuck on a setting, the only way to stop it was to smash the lock. He'd already done that, and he didn't want to go there again, and end up like his father.

Pam was also having trouble sleeping. Her wrist was throbbing and it was hard to find a comfortable position. Everything had been so relaxed at the protest, the group she had ended up with were much younger, had treated her like a mascot, fascinated by her experience of the sixties' protests and rallies she had been on. The dawn raid on Monday had been a shock and the ensuing night in a police cell followed by a day in accident and emergency had wiped her out completely. Pam had no idea what to do. Worst case scenario was calling Veronica or Ian and asking if they could drive Betsy home, or staying until her arm healed enough to drive herself. If she stayed she knew she would have to move Betsy, that idiot policeman was too close for comfort. It was still early when she heard a light tapping on the side of the Westfalia.

"Who is it?"

"Just a quick word if that's ok." It was the reporter from the news who had been interviewing protestors on Friday, Pam recognised her voice.

"I've nothing to say, please go away." As Pam sat up she realised there were several people around Betsy. What on earth they wanted was beyond her, but she would need to do something or be trapped inside all day. There was one thing she knew about the press, if they smelled even the faintest whiff of a story, they wouldn't leave well alone. But why she should interest them, she couldn't fathom. She brushed her hair, managed a quick change and opened the door, her "I have nothing to say" speech ready to go.

Whether it was the size of the crowd, the flashing of cameras or the combination of pain, painkillers and whisky, Pam had no idea why she fainted. She wasn't a fainter.

She remembered his voice telling them to back off, leave her alone and his arm stretching out under her waist to catch her fall. Propped up on a cushion with her feet up inside his flat on the brown corduroy couch, Pam tried to put the pieces together.

"Hot sweet tea," he said as he handed her a large blue mug.

"Thank you, I ...," she was about to tell him she didn't use sugar but that felt churlish. He was being kind and had in some ways rescued her. What on earth would her children say if she was splashed all over the papers or television news?

"Did they take a picture or anything do you know?" she asked.

"Well if they did, what could they say? Lady faints in front of her van, not much of a story in that. Do you often faint?"

"Never!" Her eyes flashed at the suggestion. "I'm not some feeble old woman you know."

"I do know, tough as old cheddar, is that right?" His eyes twinkled, "And I wouldn't say old woman."

Pam lowered her head, taking a large gulp of the hot sweet tea. It tasted good. Perhaps it was hunger that had made her faint, she suddenly felt ravenous. She hadn't actually eaten since being in the copse and sharing a protein bar from her bum bag with one of the other protestors on Sunday night. She had refused the choice of ham or egg salad sandwich offered by the custody Sergeant.

"I'm not being rude but would you like to have a bath or take a shower? I can make you some breakfast, I'll bet you haven't really had much to eat."

It was as if he had read her mind she thought, nodding.

"Are you sure, I mean, I don't want to take up your time, you must be busy and ..." She didn't know what else to say. The annoying and intrusive policeman had turned out to be rather kind. "My name is Pam, by the way, it seems we haven't ever exchanged names and here I am about to get naked in your bathroom."

He chuckled and put out his hand towards hers, "Geoffrey."

The water felt good running down her back. Washing in a Westfalia was doable but she hadn't even had the chance to do that since joining the protest. She had chosen the location because it was near a community centre with showers, shops and within walking distance of the protest. She hadn't expected her first shower, since leaving the bed and breakfast in Oxford, to be in a private flat. Whatever he was cooking smelled great, she hadn't had a good full English in forever, and she felt somewhat guilty that she hadn't told him she was a vegetarian, she had been expecting toast. Would the poor pig who had sacrificed its life forgive her? More to the point would Robert or Veronica?

"Impressive," Pam commented on the dining table set with orange juice, and two plates of bacon, sausage, eggs, tomato and toast. "Would you mind helping me sort this sling thing out, I seem to have twisted it at the back."

Parting her hair he managed to untie the knot that was digging into her neck.

"Thank you," she said stepping forward, the touch of his fingers had tickled and she needed a moment. He didn't seem to notice, she felt awkward.

"I wasn't sure if you were a baked beans girl, I can heat some if you'd like?"

She smiled," this is way too much and I have a confession ..."

"That you are vegetarian?" he came back beforc she could finish the sentence.

"Yes."

He went into the kitchen and came back with some packaging. Linda McCartney Sausages and a brand of non-meat bacon she had never heard of.

"It was when I went to fetch your wash bag from your van, I realised all the food you had looked like it came from a health food store, lots of non-meat protein. My wife, my dead wife, was vegetarian, so I knew what to buy."

"That's totally unexpected and amazing," said Pam. Her initial thoughts about him dissipating even further, replaced by curiosity and humility. You really can't judge a book by its cover she reminded herself, feeling admonished.

"I just hoped you weren't vegan that would have been much trickier."

Pam, tucked into the food heartily and looked around. His CD collection, books and art pieces told a very different story from the one she had assumed when they met last Friday morning, plus there were several framed photographs including those of a young girl from baby to teenager. Did he have a daughter and where was she? Pam wondered.

The silence that ensued was not uncomfortable, but Pam's curiosity soon got the better of her.

"When did you lose your wife?"

He had not expected the question and, for a moment, he wanted to shut the conversation down, change the subject. But something about her, her long wet hair, her soft grey green eyes, her calmness drew him out of himself. He told her about his wife's death, what had happened to him afterwards, not believing or accepting the accident was an accident leading to a breakdown and, in turn, the breakdown leading to his daughter living with her aunt. "She's fourteen now, poor kid. What I put her through."

Pam's eyes were filled with tears as she listened to his story. The unfurling unfairness of grief. And in his case, the rudeness of losing someone so suddenly. At least Robert had been ill, and she'd had time to prepare. She stretched out her good hand across the table, a genuine response of empathy. He put his hand over hers. The gesture took them both from comforting to desire, a release of pent up emotion that, for her, had started when he touched the back of her neck to fix the sling. Neither of them spoke as they moved from the table, consenting by responding, their coupling like a dance whose rhythm changed from intensity to gentle, accepting and giving, leading and following, slowing and hastening. He managed her gently, mindful of her wrist.

"Are you alright," he asked her, running his finger down the curve of her arm. They were laying on top of his bed, he pulled the throw over them and adjusted the pillows.

Pam turned to look at him, "I'm fine, I ..." She had no words, she was content, happy, relaxed, certainly she had no regrets about making love with him.

"Me too", he said gently as if reading her mind and agreeing with her.

"Sausages," she suddenly blurted out laughing and exaggerating the s.

He grinned, "yep, the spiciest I've had in a long time," he whispered as he leaned over to take her again.

It was noon by the time Geoffrey left the flat to continue with his police duties. Pam took another quick shower, the forgotten smell of sex was pungent. She wrapped herself in the white bath towel, cleaned away the breakfast dishes and was sitting on the couch with a purring Twinx when she heard the front door open. By the time she realised someone was in the flat it was too late to do anything about the towel and change into her dress and underwear which were still strewn about the living room.

"Who are you?" demanded the young woman Pam guessed to be Nicola, Geoffrey's daughter.

Adjusting the towel in the hope of retaining some dignity and feeling like a fourteen year old, caught out smoking behind the sheds at school, Pam introduced herself as a friend of her father's.

"It's nice to meet you," said Pam, the awkward air between them hung like a sword in mid thrust.

"He's disgusting and so are you," said Nicola, turning quickly as she headed back into the hallway, grabbing the bag she had brought with her from the second bedroom.

"Wait, please, this is all a big misunderstanding. Your Dad will be devastated if you leave and he doesn't get to see you. Please don't leave, I'm on my way out if you'll give me a few minutes to tidy up." The girl agreed, nodding sullenly, her eyes casting daggers as Pam scooped up her clothes and vanished into her father's bedroom to dress.

When Pam unlocked the Westfalia, she found several messages on her phone from Veronica, the last one "so you got arrested?" was incredulous. The events on Monday morning had made the news headlines. Pam had not been in touch with either of her children since she had left the previous Wednesday, so much had happened and, from the sound of it, Veronica had called every police station and hospital between Dulwich and the Pennines to find out what had happened to her mother. There was nothing for it but to call back straight away, try and navigate her way through Veronica's "I told you so" mindset. It had been stupid of her to forget the phone.

"Veronica, it's Mum," Pam held her breath as she listened to the loud vocalized diatribe about Pam's thoughtlessness, disregard for her family and irresponsible attitude to life in general. Veronica's brother, Ian was on his way to London on business and would be checking up on her in person by going to the park to try and find her, which he had apparently said was damned inconvenient.

"Sorry to be such a bother," said Pam not very contritely. Her daughter's outbursts had been getting worse lately and Pam wondered if she was in early perimenopause or not getting enough sex, sleep or both. Two telling offs from the younger generation in the same morning, after such a pleasurable interlude, did not make Pam particularly receptive to the woes of her children. For goodness sake it was only a week. True, she should have called but she had not intended to be sleeping in the park and she wasn't used to being hooked up to a phone all the time the way Veronica and Ian were. They carried their phones everywhere as if their lives depended on constant contact.

"How did you get arrested?" Demanded Veronica.

"Hmm, well sort of by accident," replied Pam.

"You don't get arrested by accident."

"Look, it's a bit more complicated, I have sprained my wrist, and I'm going to have to stay here for a few more days until I can put pressure on it to drive. The doctor said about three days, and it should be fine, if I keep it strapped and well rested. I'm wearing a sling, tell Poppy."

"I'm not telling Poppy anything about this Mum. Honestly, it's as if I have four children to take care of you, Poppy, Jonathan and Michael." Veronica burst into tears.

"Ah," said Pam, the expression she always used when she didn't know what to say, or knew that there was more to the story. "How is Michael?"

"I don't want to talk about it, not on the phone. I'm sorry about your wrist. Maybe ask Ian to drive you back. He will be looking for you this afternoon, about four I think he said. Why don't you call him and make the arrangement?"

Pam paused. Her son could definitely drive Betsy back, they would easily be home by ten, the way he drove.

"I'll give him a call. If you talk to him first then tell him I'm fine and really there's no need for him to drive me, I'll be on the road myself, on Saturday I should think."

"Mum!"

"Yes, I know, I'm infuriating, but there's one or two things I want to do whilst I am here. And as I've got the time off work, I might as well use it."

Pam called her son and left a message to let him know she was finc and would be in touch when she was leaving London, probably on Saturday. Ian was more level headed than Veronica, he would be relieved not to have to drive Betsy. Instead he could enjoy whatever he had had planned to do in London rather than rescuing his mother.

Pam took her phone and camera and headed back to the park. The injunction meant that the copse was protected for the time being and although there were a few protesters with signs and placards, the park was peaceful and there was no police presence. Pam wandered into the heart of the copse, she wondered if she would be able to find the exact tree and whether the heart would still be there. It didn't take her long, the dappled sunlight seemed to light her path directly to the old oak and there it was, P and R, a heart with an arrow and their initials, carved in the trunk for posterity. Pam traced the carving with her index finger and breathed in the memory once more. She smelled the wood, the grass beneath her feet, the essence of patchouli she had worn despite that its fragrance had long vanished.

After taking several pictures of the trees Pam decided to walk to East Dulwich and take a photograph of the blue plaque commemorating the flat where Enid Blyton was born in 1897. Pam doubted the story about the Magic Faraway Tree was based on the trees in the copse, given the family had moved from the area when Enid was quite young, but it was a nice thought and gave Pam an odd sense of connectivity. The now busy road still boasted trees and double fronted red brick houses of a more genteel era. Their once lush gardens paved over and the interiors turned into flats.

It was gone six when Pam returned to Betsy, she was exhausted, having walked most of the afternoon. A small white envelope was tucked under the windscreen wipers containing a handwritten note. It was from Geoffrey, asking if they could meet at The Pear Tree Pub on the corner, around seven.

Pam wondered whether Nicola was still at the flat. She wasn't sure if she wanted to meet him again, but then, if she hadn't, why had she decided to stay in London, not ask Ian to drive her home? Why was she making it complicated?

"Hello," he said as she joined him at the corner table in the pub garden. I bought a bottle of white, I hope that's okay, or would you prefer..."

"Glass of white would be lovely," she interrupted, recognising he was as nervous as she was.

"So you met Nicola then?"

"Yes, perhaps not the best introduction in the world, wearing a towel instead of clothes."

"Mmm, I hear she thinks you and I are disgusting." His eyes twinkled as he looked at her.

"Is she still there?"

"Nope, she had had a fight with my sister, stormed out to come home to me, found you and decided to go back to Val's after giving me a dressing down."

"Oh god, I'm so sorry."

"Nothing to be sorry about. I've talked to Val. Nicola has finally agreed to see a family therapist, try and get this all sorted out. I've buried my head in the sand for too long. In an odd way perhaps this will be the catalyst for change. Nicola can finally face how angry she is about her mum's death, as well as the way I let her down. The fact that I couldn't deal with her pain as well as my own."

They sipped the wine in silence after that, taking in each other with their eyes, feeling mutually at ease, understanding the pain of loss of the other. It was the most intimate Pam had ever felt with a man, other than Robert.

"Shall we go back to my place, I've a ton of veggies?"

Pam laughed, "yes please."

As soon as they arrived back at the flat, their lovemaking continued as naturally as it had started that morning. Easing and healing the grief they both felt by their combined experience of being widowed. Letting go of the physical denial of pleasure and allowing themselves the freedom to risk loving, being loved once more.

Geoffrey did not have to work until Saturday and they spent the following forty eight hours talking, walking, loving, learning and desiring each other. They laughed about the gap in their age and decided it was irrelevant, and it remained that way until Veronica showed up, unannounced, to drive her mother home.

Veronica was the quintessential victim of everyone else's thoughtlessness. In her mind, Michael not taking the rubbish out, Poppy not tidying her toys away and her mother not telephoning her were examples of wrong being done to her. A deliberate act of harm.

To Michael, Poppy, Pam and even Jonathan, Veronica's moods were simply her personality. They accepted her sounding off, did not see the anguish she felt or that she blamed them for how she felt. It would make no sense to them. But Michael was becoming tired of his wife's constant criticism and he suggested, if she was so worried, she take herself off to London to bring Pam home. It was a break they all needed. The ensuing row resulted in Veronica taking the last train to London and staying with an old university friend as her mother had, yet again, not answered her phone.

"Where the hell are you, Mother?" Veronica demanded as Pam eventually answered. She had switched it off Friday morning and only remembered to turn it back on when Geoffrey's phone started to ring whilst he was getting ready for work, after they had enjoyed an early breakfast together. Geoffrey had persuaded her to wait until Monday before she drove north, even though he would be working during the day; they could enjoy Saturday evening together and most of Sunday, unless something really bad happened.

Pam, who wasn't expected back at work until the following Wednesday, readily agreed. She booked into a B & B for Monday night to break the return journey.

"Veronica, please don't speak to me like that, what on earth's the matter?"

"Nothing is the matter with me. I'm here in London to drive you home. In case your wrist hasn't healed."

"Well, I do wish you'd checked with me darling, because I've changed my plans, I'm not leaving until Monday now. I was going to give you a call today, to let you and Ian know." The sound of silence was deafening as Veronica took in her mother's words.

Geoffrey signed to her that he had to leave and would see her later at The South Bank at seven for the concert. She nodded and waved, her brow furrowed as she waited for her daughter to speak. But as the seconds passed it was Pam who broke the silence.

"Why don't we meet for some lunch, then you can tell me why you are really here?"

Pam rightly guessed that it was not her needs that had prompted Veronica to head to London. There had been similar nights away due to rows at home last year, before they went on the break. In fact, she now wondered, if a row with Michael was the real reason Veronica and the children had stayed over at Pam's the night before her trip?

Veronica looked unusually messy when Pam saw her from a distance. Her daughter was always immaculate, in jeans, in play clothes, even when cooking, she rarely had a hair out of place. Pam and Robert had often joked that Veronica was a changeling, she was so different from them their relaxed attitude to clothing and hairstyles.

"Hello love," Pam said, putting an arm out to hug her daughter.

Pam let Veronica talk, it was what was needed and, for once, she talked without pointing the finger of blame at anyone but herself. "I've been a mean and miserable cow to him for ages." she finished up, wailing into the tissue Pam handed her to wipe her face, wet with tears and snot.

"You've been grieving my love," said Pam calmly. "You had Poppy two weeks after your dad died, then Jonathan came along, and although that was a blessing, you never had time to really grieve. You have never once talked about how you felt about your dad dying."

"Grief? You think this is grief?"

Pam nodded, "Well, not just grief. I think you know what I mean, "but Veronica shook her head.

"I'm not one of your clients you can trick into believing pop psychology, just because you say something. This isn't grief, or depression, this is about not having a proper mother. A mother who would not embarrass me by wearing alternative clothes or going off on protests."

Pam knew that there was no point in responding, Veronica was still not ready. Pam had suspected postpartum depression after Poppy and it had been worse with Jonathan. Michael had been a rock and he had confided his worries to Pam. Another man might have left, but Michael was stalwart, only now it seemed, Veronica may have gone too far even for him. This wasn't about lack of sleep, or lack of sex, her daughter was heading for a breakdown.

It was Veronica's turn to break the silence.

"So what was it that was so important you had to stay in London for?"

Pam took a breath, she didn't want to lie to her daughter. However telling Veronica she had taken a lover at this particular juncture was unlikely to do anything but pour oil on already troubled waters.

"I have a ticket for a concert, tonight. Last minute decision really." Pam felt her face starting to flush.

Veronica was curious, something about the way her mother spoke.

"And?"

"And nothing."

"Oh come on mum, I know you better than that."

The tide had turned, now it was Pam defending against something she didn't want to talk to Veronica about, but she knew she would have to. Veronica was relentless like a dog with a bone if she suspected a secret. Pam fished in her bag for her sunglasses. The sun was bright but the action bought her time.

Putting the glasses on she said, "I'm going to the concert with a new friend."

"Do you mean a man?"

"Yes, and Veronica, please don't ask me lots of questions. I don't want to tell you too much about him yet. I really don't know him that well, except that he's very kind."

"You don't know him that well, but you know him well enough to ignore your family and put them to a lot of trouble and worry about you."

Pam shook her head. "You're being a touch dramatic. Today is Saturday, I was going to call you, and Ian, to let you know I was staying on for a couple more days. You turning up in London was a surprise, and more about you than me." It was time to be honest with her daughter, stop pussyfooting around if she was really going to help her through this. Although why she chose that particular moment to decide this Pam couldn't fathom.

Veronica pushed her chair out from the table and stormed off. Pam didn't follow, there was no point, Veronica would need time to calm down and she did that best when she was left alone. Pam decided to give her an hour and then call her. But the row had upset her. Robbed her of the contentment she had been enjoying since she and Geoffrey became lovers. Perhaps it was the sun, or the fact that she was left sitting alone that she noticed all the couples sitting together, or walking past, hand in hand. Young and old but, Veronica noted, the pairs were both the same age. Was that why she hadn't wanted to talk to Veronica about him, because she was embarrassed about their age difference? It didn't matter, they agreed it didn't, or did it?

Pam was taken off guard by the sadness she felt. Sadness for the way she had quarrelled with her daughter, for Robert and now for Geoffrey. She could see it was hopeless really. Their lives were so different, his in London, hers in the Pennines and he had a young daughter to mend huge fences with. Pam would be a distraction, get in the way of what he needed to do with Nicola, making her the centre of his world until she felt secure again. Fourteen was a delicate age and Pam didn't want to be the cause of things going further off the rails. And of course, there was Veronica. Her daughter and her grandchildren were going to really need her support, if she could persuade Veronica to accept professional help, or if she didn't, the worst case, her marriage ended.

Pam called Veronica and left a long message, telling her that she had changed her mind, would leave London on Sunday, and would love to drive back together, stay overnight somewhere nice, where they could have some mother and daughter time. Pam's treat. Veronica's text pinged back, almost immediately. Yes. Thank you.

Pam braced herself for the next parting. She waited until after they made love that night to explain to Geoffrey what had happened with her daughter, how she felt about his needs and Nicola's.

"I wish it wasn't so." he said gently, he had tears in his eyes. "This has been so precious."

"And we will always have this," she said, kissing his eyes and pulling herself up to comfort him and, at the same time, comforting herself. They would always have this moment in time, a moment when two lonely people found each other, and in their finding healed the wounds of love lost.

Grace

"Once you eliminate the impossible,
whatever remains, no matter how improbable,
must be the truth" - Sherlock Homes

Arthur Conan Doyle

Grace

I allowed the azure water to cover my toes as I walked barefoot along the white sand, unconcerned that the new varnish would chip, carrying my espadrilles.

The last time I had been in Spain was with him, I had painted my toes that night too. What would he say to me now, a mature woman wearing this shade of red?"

Was it bravery or foolishness that had persuaded me to make the booking? I was thirty five, I had never been anywhere alone before and I needed to shake off that cloud of doubt that haunted me wherever I went, day and night. Stop being two people, the internal voice endlessly second guessing the external.

It was three years since my story competed for headline space in the news that The Beatles were finally breaking up. The 10th April 1970 was indelibly tattooed on my brain. Like me, their end had not happened overnight. But, on the first day of the trial, I made the headlines, and the newspaper coverage ensured my face was as recognised as theirs wherever I went. How they had born it I didn't know, but fame rather than infamy is, no doubt, a sweeter pill. Going dark from natural blonde had helped but there were those who saw beyond the bottle, usually women. The same women who now snubbed me, had once wanted to be my friend. Women who clung to their status by invitations to our house parties, and as guests at the lavish dinners he threw.

What would they have made of the boxes of photographs?

The public had only seen the ones the press thought safe enough to print, salacious and disturbing as they were. And when the others were shown to the jury, I felt like my soul had left me. I was judged at the very least complicit, at the very worst I was Eve who had tempted and swayed good men to lose their heads.

The 'good' men, whose faces haunted my dreams. If it hadn't been for Natalie, I wouldn't be here today, so ironic the mistress saving the wife, although that wasn't her plan. She, like my family, had sought to make money, I wonder if she thought her testimony would finally get me, destroy me? There were photographs of her everywhere after the trial and what they wrote was not flattering. And Charles, Alasdair's hypocrite lawyer, who could have stopped it all if only he had stepped in once he knew. At least he'd been struck off.

I returned to the small hotel my solicitor Claire had recommended, when I told her I needed to get away, to take some time to think about my future. Our roles had blurred from professional to friendship and Claire was the only person I trusted these days. When my family had tried to make money from my downfall, selling those pictures of me as a child to the tabloids, she was the first to bang them to rights. What were they thinking? And afterwards, realising I now had a fortune, pretending to care. Thanks to Claire I could see through it, and I determined never to see any of them again. I changed for dinner, it was a habit I couldn't seem to break even now. I hadn't been raised that way, I wasn't posh from the right side of Edinburgh, but his training had been precise and despite everything I wanted to let go of, to change I found it hard to step out of who I had become for him.

"Buenas noches señora."

I followed the waiter to the quiet corner table at the back of the restaurant. I could tell when I checked in that the staff were unused to an unaccompanied female traveller. My presence in the dining room caused a range of responses varying from mirth to scorn and curiosity by the waiters and other guests.

I took a book everywhere to distract myself, if only the words on the pages would penetrate my brain. Instead all I could see were the statements against me, swimming over the paper like a school of piranhas ruthlessly cornering their prey.

“Perdon senora, telefono,” the young woman from reception interrupted.

I hesitated, only Claire knew I was here and it would be unusual for her to call out of office hours. Had the press found me?

Disconcerted, I stumbled and sent the glass of rioja tumbling, the red wine soaking into the white napkin and cloth. It was the same colour as that dress. An image of me dressed in red satin flashed into my mind. I was twenty five.

I could hear his voice. “You stupid woman.”

“Lo siento,” I stammered.

Flushed, I tried uselessly to mop up the wine with my handkerchief, aware that everyone was looking. A waiter was waving his arms, attempting to stop me, two others rushed over to change the cloth and clear away the mess.

“Por favor,” the young woman was pointing to the exit.

“Telefono,” she repeated.

I followed her, to avoid eye contact I kept my head bowed, but I could feel the stares penetrating me as I walked the length of the dining room. My spine shivered, my corner table no longer a discreet hide-away. I had drawn attention to myself, the lone, almost middle-aged Scottish woman with her book. How pathetic I must have seemed.

“Hello, who is this?” I was conscious of the quiver in my voice as I spoke softly into the receiver.

“Grace, I have good news.”

I sighed, relieved it was Claire and not the press. “Good News, really?”

“Yes, Ludo has been found. He tried to go back to Glasgow and get some of his personal possessions and some money, I think. No one will believe that you aren’t completely innocent now, and of course you will be called as a witness.”

I took a sharp intake of breath. Claire had no idea of my transaction with Ludo. His reappearance was not the good news she thought.

“Thank you Claire,” the words came out as a whisper.

"Are you alright? I thought you'd be happy. That's why I called as soon as I knew, rather than waiting until tomorrow."

"Yes, sorry, thank you. I'm glad to hear from you, but I'm also scared, telling the story over and over, I'm not sure I can. Claire, it's very public in reception, can I call you tomorrow from the post office? They have booths." I needed time to think.

"Of course, Grace. Give me until two in the afternoon, that's three your time, is that alright?"

"Yes, yes, that's perfect. If, well, if I'm needed to testify do I need to come home sooner than I planned?

"No, this will all take a while. But do let me know if your plans change. You're still heading for Florence on Saturday?"

"Yes. Leg two of my European adventure, I'm not sure - ..."

"It's beautiful, you'll love it there. You'll fill your sketchbook, make new memories. One day this'll all be behind you. You'll see." Claire's confident voice challenged my doubts. Now Ludo was found, would that make things better or worse I wondered?

"Grace?"

"Yes, sorry, I hope so. Thanks for everything Claire. I'll speak to you tomorrow. I ..."

"Yes, Grace?"

"Oh, nothing, I just want to say I'm so grateful for everything you did."

"Grace, you're my client, but you're more than that. You know you are. Try and relax - you sound tense. We'll speak tomorrow."

"Fuck," I released the unfamiliar expletive under my breath, louder than I had intended. There seemed no other word. What was it my father had said when I told him I was engaged? You can take the girl out of the dung heap, but you can't take the dung out of the girl. I looked around, no one seemed to have heard or noticed.

I couldn't face going back into the dining room. I was still hungry and had left my book on the table, although perhaps that had fallen victim to the wine.

My thoughts took over. I was back at that dance, wearing the deep red halter dress with a flower in my hair. What was I thinking?

I could hardly blame Sandy, my then so-called best friend. She had egged me on to buy it, that was for certain but neither of us could have known how he would have responded. Sometimes I could still feel the taste of that awful rug in my mouth as he dragged me across it, the fibres burning my skin. How could I have known it wasn't the first time he had taken me like that, seen me taken like that? Why did I not put the bruises, the infections together? The total oblivion and missing hours when I woke up in the morning.

Our marriage had seemed like a fairy-tale. I was nineteen, he was already established and from a very different social class. I'd never been remotely easy with a boy, too scared of getting pregnant and so much more. Scared little rabbit, my sisters had called me when I was growing up. But sex was not what he was after. When I tried to tempt him before we married he'd been quite angry. How could I have known that the respectability protecting my honour was all a sham, that I was more valuable as a virgin?

I fetched my wrap from my room. There was a bar that served food a short walk away. I could be anonymous there. I took the drawing pad that, along with my selection of books, distracted me and prevented conversations with strangers, who I was sure would see through me or guess. My Spanish was good, not as fluent as my French but I pretended that I couldn't speak it, save for my error at dinner after spilling the wine. Did they notice?

I used to translate for him: he liked showing me off like that. It made him look modern, to include his wife in his business, but when I was not translating I learned to be mute, dutiful, demure. He hated it if he thought I was showy, yet, he liked showy women, encouraging them, flirting with them in front of me, in front of their husbands.

I'm back to the dress, that stupid, stupid dress with its spaghetti straps and wrap over skirt. He unravelled it in an instant, asked me what the hell I thought I was doing, ignoring the classic Lagerfeld he'd picked out for me to wear. Made up like a tramp, he said, did I not know only cheap women and whores wore red varnish? And he would know. The words still stung, worse than the slaps, and that final humiliation. Only two people knew what really happened that night and one was dead.

When Charles called by our villa the next morning with papers for Alasdair to sign I knew he saw the dress lying torn where I had kicked it behind the chair, my bruised eye, and the limp. Charles made no response to my pathetic request for help. He couldn't wait to get away.

"Marital problems are not my business Grace." How cold his words were.

I had attempted to clean up but my wrists were sore and I was woozy from the medication he had given me before he went to play golf. I had tried to refuse, I hated the way it made me feel.

'It's for your own good Grace, you know that. There's a good girl." And of course, I complied. After all, if I hadn't worn that dress, he wouldn't have treated me like that, but I didn't really know. How could I have?

Focus, Grace, I told myself as I arrived at the bar. I hesitated, this was far beyond my comfort zone. I was about to leave, go back to the hotel when she caught my arm.

"Grace? Grace McKay?"

Oh my god, my stomach churned over, I wanted to be sick, certain it was a journalist.

"Please leave me alone." My words were hardly assertive and I wasn't surprised that she didn't let me go.

"Grace, it's me, it's Sandy."

"Sandy?"

I looked up slowly, and there she was. They say that if you think about someone you haven't seen or heard from you will meet them or hear about them, I had never believed it, well I suppose I hadn't really had cause to put it to the test. She had hardly changed, she still had that open-faced friendly expression that had drawn me to her, long before I met him. We were both fair and sometimes people even thought we were sisters.

“Come and sit with me - I’m meeting some friends but they’re late as usual.” She laughed, the way she had when we were in that market, the day she saw the dresses, one in white, the other deep red.

“Let’s get them, Grace, let’s show them what we can do on the dance floor. Your Alasdair will take notice of you wearing this, get his eyes off that showy piece in the black bikini.”

Her words rang in my head as if it were yesterday.

“I can’t stay here Sandy. I’m sorry.” I pulled hard against her grip and ran out into the night. The sun had set but the beach walk, cafes, and bars were still busy.

“Grace, wait. I just want to find out how you are. The way you disappeared after that night .... I’ve so often thought about you. I’ve missed you.”

“Disappeared? What are you talking about?”

And there it came, a tidal wave of resentment that I had harboured for almost ten years.

“Sandy, the day I needed a friend most of all, you didn’t come. I saw you chatting to Charles. You were both laughing. I left the next day as planned, so no I didn’t just disappear. I wrote to you, but nothing back. What a friend you turned out to be.”

Sandy stared at me, her mouth open, a stupefied expression on her face.

We had known each other since we started school. When we graduated Sandy moved to London to train as an air hostess. I stayed put and got married, but we stayed in constant touch. I loved her postcards from far flung places and she enjoyed my carefully composed long winded letters. She shared a flat off the Kings Road and became an “it” girl, even featured in Cosmo when they did a story about glamour and career. Our worlds couldn’t have been more different. It was a complete fluke she had been at the same villa complex on holiday, but he thought we had planned it. Of course for him the trip was all business, legal business and making more and more money.

The day Sandy suggested we go and buy the dresses was the most fun thing I had done in ages. The freedom of getting dolled up, painting each other's nails, I was so happy. Sandy had seen the way he looked at other women, the ones who dressed like I dressed that night, for him, I wanted him to love me, desire me, not just a wife to a cold formal husband doing his duty and, truth be told, I hoped to get pregnant again despite my GP's warning after the last miscarriage. I felt I was over it, and hoped I could stop taking the pills.

I had always been shy and awkward. Sandy was fun, full of ideas. I was the bookworm who helped her with homework. Reading the classics, learning three languages, because I wanted to. The introvert and the extrovert, we were an odd pair, but we loved each other deeply, or I thought we had. Her words cut through my memories like a knife. Like that knife.

"I wrote to you too, the letters came back unopened. I wanted you at my wedding. You didn't just hurt me by your silence, Grace. You hurt my mum too. She was there for you when yours died. I saw you just once after Spain, passing through Heathrow. I waved. Maybe you didn't see me, but he did. I was in uniform, did I just look like "staff"?"

Her words winded me, the erect spine I had constructed crumbled, the colour drained from my face, it was like finding the photographs all over again. Those wretched images of me, subjugated. I had seen her, but he had clamped my arm, daring me to acknowledge her.

More secrets, more lies, I didn't know how much more I could bear. I needed to get somewhere quiet where I could breath. The esplanade was getting busier, rowdier - this was no place for the conversation that needed to be had.

Sandys flat was like her, colourful, full of energy with big bold paintings hung randomly over the white walls. So different from the formal home I had shared with him in Morningside, Edinburgh.

"I just couldn't stand grey little Britain any longer. Once I was divorced Spain beckoned and I answered. Cheers." Sandy clinked her glass against mine.

I swallowed, looking at her, she seemed so carefree, at one with the world. She had always been like that, I hated myself for being envious, but I couldn't help it. At that moment I wanted to be anyone but me.

"So Grace ..."

"You really don't know?"

"Know what - I mean, you're not with him, so, I'm guessing we're both divorced."

"He's dead."

"Ah, I'm sorry, I'm not sorry. Except I am sorry for you." Her words tumbled out.

"I was on trial for killing him."

The silence that followed was deafening. Sandy held my gaze, lost for words, no quip or comeback fell from her lips.

"Aren't you going to ask me if I did it?"

She nodded, a Pavlovian response.

"Not Proven. The Bastard verdict."

"And that means....?" Her face was a picture.

I wanted to laugh. The irony that I suddenly was more interesting than she could ever have imagined. Interesting? My inner voice questioned. Is that how you see yourself now? It's better than feeling like a victim. I quickly shut down the thought. I needed to remain composed. It was what I'd learned to do. That debacle in the hotel earlier was not me, I could not be that again.

"Grace, I'm not going to judge you, whatever happened, whatever you did or didn't do, I am your friend and despite such a long gap, I will always be your friend. He was a bastard, I could see that."

"But you and Charles, the way you were laughing that morning?"

"Charles is a fool, he thinks he's charming and I'm a good pretender. But I'm guessing he did fool me that morning. He told me that he'd accidentally seen more than he should, that's why I didn't come over to your villa. According to Charles you were in the middle of an erotic second honeymoon. I guessed the dress had worked."

"He raped me."

Sandy looked at me the way Claire had when I first told her what had happened. Wondering how a married woman could be raped, if she had been trying to seduce her husband by wearing a sexy dress.

"I know, it doesn't make any sense, it didn't to me either, until I found out what had really been going on. To the outside world I was the demure dutiful wife. But behind closed doors, I was his prize to share, it was a sick secret. I still keep asking myself how I could not have known. My dreams are dark, and I am afraid to fall asleep, in case it happens again. It's irrational now, but you can't unsee what you've seen. I wish I could."

"I'm completely lost, we need food and more wine," said Sandy suddenly standing up, her face drained of colour. I recognised the response, my secret was too shocking even for her. Except, it turned out that it wasn't.

"I can't believe that he put you through all that." She said, cradling me in her arms later. I had been talking for over an hour.

"Me and Natalie, although of course she entered into it all willingly at first. She thought it was fun and they paid her well, but like they had with me, they got tired of the same pet. She was nineteen when they recruited her, I was nineteen when he married me. I must have been about twenty five when I was unknowingly retired from service, from the way I looked in the photographs anyway. Six years of being raped by a group of men, one of them being my husband."

"And the doctor, he was part of it?"

"Yes, both the psychiatrist he made me see and the GP. But of course no one believed me about that or that I didn't know what was going on, despite the miscarriages, the medical history of infections and the pills. What Natalie said about them didn't count either, because she was paid for her services. She was really hung out to dry by the prosecution and the press. Now Ludo is back, perhaps the doctors and the others will get charged. I don't know. They're all so respectable, covering up for each other. Although they were happy to let Charles take the fall."

"So this Ludo coming back, it's all good?"

I looked at her and shrugged.

"In one way", I said slowly, "but there is a catch."

"Go on," prompted Sandy.

"You see, I found out what was going on when they were using Natalie. Alasdair had bought me a really expensive bracelet with a heart clasp on our fifth wedding anniversary. He had it engraved with his initials and a heart. He bought her a bracelet, with the same engraving. I thought it was a complete accident when we met in the ladies toilet at the opera, but she had somehow manoeuvred it. She showed me the bracelet, she had thought he was going to leave me for her. It was her attempt to force the issue. She didn't realise how complex he was and a hypocrite. Divorce would be the last thing he would permit, to ruin his respectable image. Perhaps that's why they ended things with her."

Sandy studied me, I knew what she was going to say. The same question I had asked myself.

"I don't mean to be judgey here but, when you found out about her, why didn't you leave him?"

"Indeed. Why didn't I? That's what the prosecution said. They built their whole case against me as an evil sexual accomplice and murderer around the fact that I must have known everything. Ludo came to me, he showed me a box of photographs of me, they were horrible, and there were other girls in them. Honestly Sandy, you couldn't tell from the way they were taken that I was not conscious. He said the images would compel them to find me guilty. I didn't know then that he was the one who arranged for the other girls, the ones that no-one believed existed. Ludo told me that one hundred thousand would keep his mouth shut and he would destroy the photographs, so I paid him. My solicitor and the barrister have no idea about any of that. As to why I didn't leave Alasdair once I knew about Natalie, I don't know. I loved him, he said he was going to stop, that she would be the last but deep down I knew he hadn't. I didn't know what he and the others were really involved in. What they did to those other girls. Not until afterwards. I promise you."

"What are you going to do Grace?"

"I don't know. I know I don't want to go back to court, relive all that all over again."

It was almost dawn by the time I left Sandys flat. We had talked through the night. I could feel the plan Sandy suggested forming in my mind as I walked back to the hotel. It was not the one I had discussed with Claire, but money was no object. Sandy was right, it meant that I could almost do whatever I wanted. I knew I didn't want to give more money to Ludo, or face the fact that he had not destroyed those other photographs. I didn't have to go back to a trial which, whatever Claire said, I could only see ending up ruining me. I could follow Sandy's example, choose somewhere else to live. I need never set foot in Edinburgh again. But I'd need time if I were to really get away and with Sandy's help it could just work.

I slept badly, tossing and turning, Ludo's face haunting me every time I shut my eyes. I was a fool to trust him after everything I knew about him. Clearly he was looking for more money, looking for me, why else would he have risked going back? I hated meeting him, doing a deal with the devil, a dirty, scurrilous waste of space. The plan that had seemed so possible and elevated me, seemed hopeless, shot to pieces. Now Ludo was arrested, he could say anything. I had turned a blind eye to evil, but I didn't know then that I was one of the flies trapped in that web.

I checked my watch. It was almost seven, I had eight hours before I was due to speak to Claire, I needed to pull myself back together. She couldn't know what I knew, and I respected her too much to put her in a professional no-win situation. I called Sandy, was our plan hopeless?

The post office was jammed with people when I arrived.

"Grace?"

"Yes, finally. Sorry it's really busy here, Claire. I had to wait ages for a booth and for the call to go through."

"It's no bother. You sound better than you did last night. I was really worried about you."

"Yes, I'm sorry I panicked. I thought it was the press. It was stupid."

"I shouldn't have called so late, out of office hours, I didn't think. But look Grace here is your opportunity to tell your story again, this time, with evidence to support everything you said, that you had no idea what had happened."

"And if it doesn't work?"

"What do you mean?"

"Could I be tried again?"

"Why would you be tried again?"

"If Ludo's evidence somehow incriminated me ... ?"

"How could it Grace? You did nothing wrong, you won't be on trial."

"I don't want to risk it Claire, sorry. I've told the story too many times, I can't face all that again. The papers, the television people showing up, which you know they would."

"You'll have no choice Grace, they will subpoena you to appear. I can't see any way around that. From what I can gather Ludo is facing some pretty heavy charges, so you're right, the press and television will be all over you again. He was crazy to think he could come back without being arrested. There was too much evidence and the other girls' statements, oh my God. What they said he did. I can't believe Charles acted for him. Let me know when you arrive in Florence and we can chat then, I have some restaurant and gallery tips for you. Try not to worry. I'm sorry you aren't as buoyed up by the news as I thought you'd be."

"It's alright. Thanks."

"Grace, are you still there?"

"Yes, but there's a queue. I'd better go. Was there anything else?"

"No, Grace, that was it. Are you sure everything is alright?"

I put down the receiver. I knew she could tell something was wrong. Was it what I said or the way I said it? She was good. I couldn't risk any association with Ludo and more fool him for returning. He wouldn't get anything more from me. I was more determined than ever about that.

I let the concierge know I would be leaving the hotel the following morning and arranged for a taxi to the airport. The sooner this was done the better. Sandy was waiting for me and, for the first time in three years, I was looking forward to having dinner with a true friend. Albeit one I might never see again.

"All set?"

"Yes, are you sure you want to help? It's not too late if you've changed your mind."

She reached out her hand and placed it over mine.

"I let you down once, Grace. I'm not about to do it again."

"The hair dye worked."

"Yes, we're the same colour, again! Don't worry it's all going to work out."

When the taxi pulled up at the hotel the next morning, I stood and watched her go. She was right, it was all going to work out. Even I couldn't tell she wasn't me. Being dark suited her. I fingered the shoulder length wig It was too close to my own colour to get away with for long, but it should get me on a plane with Sandy's passport. Claire wouldn't be fooled of course if she tried to reach me. Sandy's easy going way of speaking would give it away. Claire was too good a listener, but if everyone thought I was in Florence it should buy me enough time.

Of course there was another choice. I stared out at the blue ocean. I hadn't even hinted to Sandy that I had a plan B, or she would never have agreed to go. They say drowning is a pleasant death, but how could they know? I wasn't a good swimmer so the tide would take me easily releasing me from the torment of knowing things I could never forget.

Time's up, Grace, my inner voice prompted. Time to choose. I walked back to Sandy's flat slowly, considering Sandy's question.

The question that I had asked myself time after time after time.

"Did you kill him, Grace?"

And my response, spoken slowly, as if I were the judge.

"It was not proven, the Bastard verdict."

It was a heavy sentence. Too heavy to live with? I simply didn't know

Fresh Compost

"Perhaps when we find ourselves wanting everything, it is because we are dangerously close to wanting nothing."

Sylvia Plath

Fresh Compost

Surrey 1966

He held the firearm steady, pointed at her forehead. The military training had never left him, but he had not expected to be using it like this.

She didn't move. Frozen to the spot, not believing he would pull the trigger, she fell straight back as the bullet made a clean entry between her eyes. Quickly, he wrapped the plastic around her head and carried her out of the house and placed her in the prepared grave in her beloved vegetable beds. He covered her with fresh compost. He arranged her, face up toward the sky. There were foxes and wildlife not averse to a fresh corpse. He doubted the police would call about the sound of the motorbikes and anyway, he had to believe Chatham's men were good, that they knew how to clean up. There would be no reason for the police to look here for the body, once they found her burned out car..

The codicil would come into play when she was pronounced dead. The property, held in trust until her death, would be inherited by a distant cousin, Stephen Monaghan, architect.

"Goodbye my dear, now you and your precious land can be at one, the way you always wanted."

Chatham was staring at him. It was difficult to tell if he was impressed by what he had witnessed or if his impassive face was because he was used to seeing death at such close quarters. They had both had a reason to want her gone from their lives, and now she was.

.oOo.

Cologne 1939

"Greta, you must help me."

Her mother's face was panic stricken as four year old Greta sat sulkily on her bed clutching her brown rabbit, refusing to move.

Her mother knew Greta didn't understand why her father had not come home and was upset about being told they were leaving, but they simply had to go. The articles Greta's father had written and published had put them all in danger.

"Come on Greta, I've made room for you in the pram, you won't have to walk."

"I'm not a baby."

"Yes, but we have a long way to go and... .."

There was a loud knock on the door. Greta's mother stiffened, she placed one of her fingers to her lips indicating to Greta to be silent. But the knocking continued and the twins, swaddled in the pram, woke up and started to cry.

"Öffne die Tür"

"Öffne die Tür" the voice repeated, demanding the door be opened.

"Einen Augenblick", Greta's mother removed her outdoor coat and opened the door.

"Ja?"

Two of Ordnungspolizei pushed past her and started their search, a third stood at the door. They did not speak and Greta's mother did not dare ask what it was they wanted; she already knew, thanking her lucky stars she had had the foresight to burn her husband's notebooks as soon as he was arrested. She just hoped they wouldn't look too closely at the pram and her clothes into which she had hidden crusts of bread and milk in preparation for the almost four hundred mile walk to Lucerne.

The officers left nothing untouched, except for the pram, even Greta's bed was turned over and stripped. By the time they left with the typewriter and some books, the flat was in chaos. They handed her some papers; she wasn't forbidden to leave the city but the papers included a signed order that said she must remove nothing from the flat; they told her they would return.

"Now, Greta please," but the child needed no cajoling, the sight of her toys and clothes being ransacked had shocked her. She held up her bunny, her large eyes filled with tears.

"Alright," her mother agreed, "yes you can bring Bunny."

The walk to Strasbourg where Greta's grandmother lived took almost four days. Her mother hadn't dared risk the train, partly because she needed to conserve the little cash she had and partly because of the officials and checks. She was terrified she would give away the real purpose for travelling and put her own mother at risk of arrest, simply by being related. By the time they arrived in Strasbourg they were exhausted and very hungry. After resting for two days they set off on the most dangerous part of the journey, crossing the border into Switzerland. In the rush to leave, Greta's bunny lay forgotten on the floor of her grandmother's home. Greta's mother refused to turn back once Greta realized Bunny was not in the pram. She opened her mouth to scream but no sound came out.

Although Greta remembered little else about that night walk, but her mother's desperation, the memory of constant hunger and thirst and a fear of being found out haunted her in different ways. Her mother was often sick as a result of the pregnancy, only found out about after her father's arrest and Greta, at four, sometimes felt like she was the mother and had to manage things beyond her years. Greta never felt satisfied, constantly looking over her shoulder in case everything she had would disappear, be taken off her somehow. But she learned to manage the overwhelming panic attacks, when her heart felt like it would explode. She learned to survive and protect herself by not showing her feelings, being distant, planning every move with caution and methodology. When she responded to the needs of her younger siblings while her mother was working it was done efficiently, without warmth.

Their in-laws in Lucerne had not been particularly thrilled to find the ragged family on their doorstep. Greta's father was somewhat of a black sheep, having turned his back on the banking profession of his father, brother, uncles and grandfather, electing to write poetry, short stories and critical analyses of the world as he saw it. His choice of wife, a German girl who was neither a beauty, wealthy, nor an intellectual disappointed them further. But they took her in and provided her and the children with a small summerhouse. There was a wood stove and running water but no formal bathroom or separate space for living and sleeping. While her mother was out working as a seamstress, making good old dresses and whatever else the families who hired her bid her to do, Greta was left alone with the twins and told to be still and quiet, under the watchful eye of the cook in the kitchen in the main house. When Elle was born, Greta's mother took her with her for the first year but after that she too became Greta's responsibility, to keep quiet, rock to sleep and feed.

By the time Greta was ten she had won round her grandfather's initial rejection of her. He still took little interest in her mother, the boys and Elle apart from extending and improving their living quarters, but for Greta it seemed he would do anything. He spent time with her and finally offered to pay for her to be privately educated. Greta looked a lot like his own daughter and he was intrigued by the quiet girl who taught herself to read books beyond her years, who was good at math and science. It was the end of the war and, despite Switzerland's neutrality, opportunities for schooling had been limited to what was available locally. He suggested sending her to England to a private boarding school when she turned eleven which coincided with Benenden School re-opening its doors in Kent. Benenden was where her father's sister had been educated. The honour and opportunity of what she was being offered was not lost on Greta who overrode her mother's objections and grabbed the chance to change her destiny with zest and determination. It was September 1946 when Greta said her final goodbye to her mother and siblings. The timing was fortunate because a year later her grandfather died. He had provided for Greta's education in his will but, at eighteen, she knew she would be on her own.

Greta studied hard, became fluent in perfectly enunciated English in the style of the day, along with the French and German she had learned as a young child. She chose friends that were well connected. Greta made use of those connections and, as soon as she graduated, landed a well-paid position as personal secretarial assistant to an executive at an international investment bank. The position opened doors into a society where opulence and plenty thrived and it was where she first met Oscar Thornberry, architect, rising star and peer of the realm. Greta was twenty one and Oscar thirty six.

Oscar was not the first client whose desire she had captured. Using her quick wit, charm and intellect, she had encouraged several hopeful suitors to open charge accounts for her at Liberty and other London stores. And, when her alluring promises failed to materialise and an account was closed, it wasn't too long before another one opened. Greta had marriage in mind, not for her the role of mistress and someone else's cast off or hand me downs.

Oscar had never married and was regarded as something of a catch. He was shy and had not fathomed the art of courtship. Greta's presence, as she collected him from reception, her perfect hourglass figure clad in pencil skirt, blouse and heels hypnotised him to the point of bumbling helplessness. The tubes containing architectural plans fell out of his arms and clattered to the floor. She did not offer to help and looked on amused, as he scrambled on all fours.

Oscar had the advantage of looks as well as money, and being a bachelor. He was also younger than most of the others. Oscar had been featured in a Sunday spread and Greta researched him thoroughly before suggesting him to her employer as a potential candidate for the new London building. She was curious as to why he wasn't married and wondered if his age could be a problem, that he would want children. She had no desire to be a milk sop to a needy baby, she'd had enough of looking after children.

Mesmerized and captivated by who he thought Greta was, Oscar didn't stand a chance. Six months later, Greta accepted his proposal and the satisfactorily large diamond cluster which she had suggested and which he thought he had chosen. She wanted to stay in London, after all Oscar had business in the House. When he told her about the land he had purchased near his parents' home and on which he wanted to build them a family home, she paid little notice and flung herself into planning a grand wedding. Oscar suggested a quiet ceremony at the local church near his parents, but he gave in to Greta's dream of a London wedding and allowed her the run of it. Invitations to the great and the good were sent and when Oscar's parents were killed in a car crash three weeks before the nuptials, she simply erased them from her table plan.

"Shouldn't we postpone everything?" he asked her on the day of the crash.

"Why? Would it bring back your parents? What about all the expense, and our honeymoon? Everything is booked." Greta knew he would not argue with her and he didn't.

She was right, he thought. It wouldn't change anything and his mother had been genuinely pleased that he was finally getting married. His parents had only met Greta twice, both times in London. He knew his mother had longed for grandchildren and now, albeit posthumously, he could at least provide her with that once he and Greta were married. Why postpone it and ruin everything for his lovely Greta?

Greta did not accompany him to the funeral pleading a headache; she spent the day alone in bed.

Ten years later, Lady Greta Thornberry strode across her lawn to inspect the new and freshly composted raised vegetable beds behind the terrace. It was a clear spring morning - Greta's favourite time of year. The promise of halcyon days boasted early buds and blossoms, a light breeze lifting her carefully coiffed hair as she inspected the work and nodded approval at Michael, her live-in handyman and gardener.

"How are the children?" Greta's question was curt, a hint of her displeasure that he had been busy with family issues when she called him to discuss the beds. The tension between them lingering like an exhaled breath contaminated by the odour of excess gluttony.

Greta's unreasonable demands and last minute urgency had crossed the unspoken boundary that existed between them.

Her land was everything. She knew no other priority. Whilst Greta loathed the house her husband Oscar had designed and built for them when they married, she was passionate, with an intensity rivalling Scarlett O'Hara, about the five acres of land that came with the property, bordering the villages of Deepwater and Littlewater. In her mind nothing was more important. Sick children didn't feature.

"They're getting better now, thank you for asking." The unsubtle sarcasm mirrored in his deep brown eyes as he looked at her.

"Good, well hopefully you'll be more available, less difficult to contact when I need you."

She turned abruptly and walked back to the house.

The award-winning, post-war glass and concrete mass that Oscar had built was regarded as a carbuncle by traditionalists and a tribute to modernism by others. Greta described it as a monstrosity. His design of the home had not been the only aspect of their marriage that had divided them. Oscar had dreamed of a family home filled with children and laughter, but Greta had other ideas. She wanted money but, more than that, she wanted recognition in her own right. Being simply wealthy did not sate her need to forget what it was once like to have absolutely nothing.

Oscar's early attempts to support and offer her advice were in vain. Greta resisted even listening to his ideas. By the end of the second year of their marriage, Oscar had retreated as she converted the once wild habitat into a successful market garden and livery stables business. Greta charged premium prices for the preserves and compost she produced. At first her customers were all local gardeners and the village store, but within five years she had ramped up production to supply orders from some of the bigger nurseries and gift shops. She became well known for her formidable negotiation skills. And now, finally, when Greta thought she could realise her plans to put herself on the map as a serious businesswoman and entrepreneur, there was another hitch.

"Damnable man," she cursed as she checked her watch and headed back to the house to change for the meeting with the solicitor. She was exasperated by how long things had taken to proceed since Oscar's death. With the exception of the solicitor finally releasing funds for the new Jaguar Sports Saloon - a negotiation which, in her opinion, had taken up too much time and energy - Greta resented the paltry allowance she was allowed until the estate was settled.

She drove with her usual speed to the village and swept into the solicitor's office, paying scant heed to the invitation by the receptionist to take a seat.

"Infuriating, meddling idiot! Even from the grave!" Greta shouted unceremoniously at Mr. Wilson, the mild-mannered family solicitor, as he read the codicil to the will.

"When did he do this? How could you have let him?"

Mr. Wilson removed his glasses and wiped his forehead. Greta was a force majeure he did not feel competent to battle with. She appeared to have forgotten that the house had been registered under Oscar's business as a separate entity for taxation purposes. Hence, it was not hers outright to do with as she pleased, now that he was finally pronounced dead.

"I will contest this. You are an imbecile."

"Mrs. Thornberry..."

"Lady Thornberry, or have you forgotten that too? Just because he's dead does not diminish my status. I retain the title."

"Excuse me, Lady Thornberry, there is also the matter that the house is registered as historically significant but you do retain full rights to do what you please with the land beyond the garden parcel."

Realising that despite her best efforts, her husband's will could now force that ugly monstrosity to remain, Greta was in high dudgeon by the time she arrived back at the house.

"Fucking bastard," she said later that afternoon to Evelyn, after three large gin and tonics on the terrace. "Years of planning down the sodding drain. I'm so fed up trying to survive without money and means." The profanity slipped from her lips with ease, she didn't have to pretend in front of Evelyn.

Evelyn nodded. She knew better than to try and pacify or argue with Greta when she was in this type of mood. Evelyn was Greta's only real friend. A patient and kind soul, Evelyn remained loyal as Greta's bridge to any form of social contact with the village since Oscar was presumed drowned almost eighteen months ago.

Oscar had been well loved, growing up in the family home in Little Water, attending the infant, junior and grammar schools in Deep Water. The family had lived in Little Water, when they moved South for work from Scotland at the beginning of the twentieth century. Oscar was somewhat shy as a child and as he grew his passion, diligence and mastery for architecture and design had left him little time for socialising and courtship even when he returned home on leave after being called up when he turned eighteen. He had preferred his own company and had not attended the dances put on by the Church. Even so, there were several disappointed hearts when Oscar eventually found someone outside the villages to marry. The 'surprise' that he was building for his bride- to-be had been the constant buzz in the pub, local shops and the endless tea parties at the heart of village life. The locals did their best to welcome Greta.

When the house was finally ready, and the day of Greta's long awaited first appearance arrived, everyone turned out to welcome her as if she were the Queen herself. Handmade bunting, tables laden with sandwiches, scones and cakes - even the school band. But Oscar's dark blue Rover swept past them on its way to the house, and neither Greta nor Oscar returned to participate in the celebrations.

A hand written note in Oscar's distinctive cursive, stating that Greta had been taken ill on their journey from London made its way around the village the following day. The letter set the gossip going and, unbeknownst to Greta, the news that a birth would soon be expected. No one then minded she had missed the welcome tea, after all morning sickness was the precursor of a blessing; but no baby came and Greta remained absent from all the village social activities. She and Oscar learned to weave around each other and for the next five years, from the outside, their marriage looked just like any other.

In August 1961, Oscar travelled to Scotland for a fishing trip. Two days later his boat was found in pieces following an explosion. The remains were dashed against the rocks on the north coast of Scotland. Greta had refused to go with him, stating she hated Scotland and saw no point in a holiday together to celebrate their fifth wedding anniversary; she had too much business to get on with. His body was never found and it was assumed by the investigators that the sea had provided Oscar with a watery grave. What little that was left of the boat gave no clues as to why the explosion had happened.

The differences in Scottish and English law concerning his death resulted in the estate being tangled up in legal limbo. Greta insisted on the appointment of a new and expensive Scottish advocate to fight her corner, claiming poverty if the estate was not dealt with. In point of fact her business was thriving but the facade of poverty was a sham which suited her. Greta had everything she had worked so hard for, except the freedom to do as she pleased financially and Greta didn't like being thwarted.

The afternoon sun started to slip behind the house and the terrace was cooling off.

"I'm going for a hack on Noble. The grey mare is a good ride if you want to join me." Greta said, draining her glass.

"Thanks, not up for it today if you don't mind. Too much gin and sun." Evelyn replied.

"Suit yourself. Don't forget dinner on Friday. Be bloody boring given they are grocers but needs must if the business is going to survive. Jim's coming so there will be some repartee to be had."

Evelyn smiled. She hadn't seen Jim since Christmas. There'd been a lot more than repartee that night. Jim had known Greta since before she was married. The brother of an old school friend, he was like a sad lap dog that could be relied upon to amuse guests, make up numbers and do party tricks. It was clear he adored Greta and however meanly she treated him he ran back for more. But Greta had gone too far last Christmas and the trick she had played on him had gone badly wrong. Jim stormed out of the house, vowing never to return. However, his bruised ego and pride healed and he sent Greta an enormous hamper from Fortnum and Mason just after New Year. Greta, being Greta, did not accept the apology for several months and kept him hanging, refusing to take his calls or respond to his letters. Now Jim was back where she wanted him, suitably punished and contrite. It was her cruelty that made him leave and her cruelty that drew him back.

Poor Jim, thought Evelyn.

Greta shuddered, she felt cold suddenly.

"Are you alright Greta?" Evelyn stretched out her arm to steady her friend. "Too much gin perhaps?"

"I'm fine, just a ghost." Greta said, but her face belied the confidence of her words.

"Are you still going for that hack?" Evelyn asked as she fixed her wrap, preparing to leave.

"Yes, I'll see you Friday."

.oOo.

Six hundred and thirty five miles away in a clinic in Lucerne the unusually large number of discharged patients settling accounts and trying to organise transport at the same time was creating a furore around the front desk of the clinic.

"Stephen, Stephen."

Nessie pushed her way through the crowd. He looked up from the paperwork he was signing and smiled. His white teeth gleaming.

"Darling girl. You got away. Thank goodness, I was so worried. Let's get out of here as fast as we can."

"You look wonderful," she said. "The photos you sent didn't do you justice."

"I feel it, and even more so now you are here; was it difficult to manage?"

"Same sick friend in the North," she laughed. "And this time, no children to be managed."

He stooped and kissed her, embracing her closely, as if he would never let her go and for them both, anxious to arrive in their room for some privacy, the lift seemed to take forever. A little while later, after they had made love, Stephen looked at himself closely in the bathroom mirror. His skin was still smooth for a man of his age and the dental treatments had given him a smile worthy of a matinee idol. He decided to stay with grey hair - Nessie said it made him look distinguished. He had hated the dark wig he used after the fire, and hair dye, even one close to his original shade, would look fake. The surgeons had been expensive, but extremely skilled, the skin grafts were near perfect, he really couldn't believe just how good he looked.

Stephen opened a second bottle of the Grand Cru. They took their glasses out onto the balcony overlooking Lake Lucerne.

"Cheers, my darling," Nessie nuzzled against him as she clinked her glass against his.

"Slainte Mhath."

He had had a choice of clinics but Lucerne suited his purpose. He could be anonymous there, a writer carrying out research on banking and the families that controlled the banks during and just after the war. His curiosity about what had really happened to Greta, where she was really from had got the better of him. The poor wretched woman he had met, Greta's mother, shocked him. She was so different from Greta and so grateful for the tiny gift he gave her. He had felt bad lying about who he was, she seemed so kind, the dissimilarity between her and her daughter evident in her love for her grown up children and even now, the missing daughter whom she had never heard from or been able to find. It was unlikely she or anyone would go looking for Greta now. His plan was safe.

.oOo.

Whilst Stephen and Nessie had been making love in Lucerne, Greta pushed her horse hard to expunge whatever was troubling her but she couldn't shake it off. Michael was working in the stables when she arrived back. He was sweaty, his chest glistening after the work he had put in getting the horse boxes ready for the show on Sunday. He knew what she wanted, her eyes flashing with anger had looked at him hungrily as she took off her helmet and shook out her dark curly hair. He pushed her onto one of the hay bales.

"Shake a leg boy, or do I need to use this?' She picked up the riding crop and swished it through the air, bringing it hard against her jodhpur clad thigh.

He grabbed the crop and flipped her over, striking her firmly with it on her buttocks. She laughed.

"Harder man, I'm not made of candyfloss."

Swish, the crop landed on her again. She pushed down her jodhpurs and raised herself up.

"Fuck me. Hard" she demanded.

Although Greta was glamorous she wasn't really his type, but she was wild and she liked it rough which his wife did not. She was also childless and the first time he took her he was pleasantly surprised to find she had kept herself well exercised in all the right places, unlike his wife,, after pushing out the twins.

"It's the riding, dahling," she'd said mockingly when he remarked on her tightness.

Most of the time their coupling was in the stables but since she'd been widowed she had invited him up to the house on a few occasions and once to a swanky suite in a hotel near the county show. They never kissed, she avoided that type of intimacy with him. She gave the orders and he obliged in whatever way she wanted him. It was a perk of sorts and certainly she paid him well for the work he did in the stables and with the garden. His son Andrew had nearly caught them at it once and it had taken a lot of pocket money to stop him telling tales to his mother. He sometimes wondered if Greta had other lovers. That fellow Jim perhaps? It didn't bother him except when she behaved like she had that morning. He knew she was capable of turning everything he had on its head. Ruining his future plans. It was bad timing that Nessie had taken off to take care of her sick friend and leave him with all the children. He didn't understand it, she had never left them before.

Michael had worked for Oscar's family since he left school. He had been fifteen, he didn't know how to do anything else, just working land and tending horses. He loved them almost as much as Greta did and had been glad of the offer of work as a handyman and a tied cottage after Oscar's parents had died. The cottage and the flexible hours had been a godsend, Greta's plans were a bonus and he soon became her right hand instead of Oscar's. His son had been six and there was another on the way. Twins had been a shock, but thanks to the peppercorn rent, Michael had been able to put a lot by, enough for the boy to go to college or university if he wanted to. There was also almost enough saved to buy a small rental property near the sea. He and Nessie would move there when he retired. Life was good.

It was late Sunday night, after the horse show when Greta first heard the motorbikes. There seemed to be three or four of them riding up and down outside on the road into the village. Despite being set back from the road their irritating buzzing penetrated her open bedroom window. It was gone one in the morning when she decided to call the police to demand them to put a stop to it.

"Useless lot," Greta complained to Evelyn the following day.

"Michael heard them too but the police said there was no sign of motorbikes anywhere, not even marks on the road to suggest there had been any. I didn't bloody well imagine it."

The next night Greta heard them again.

"The motorbikes are back," she barked down the telephone to the patient constable on duty. He apologised and stated that due to staff shortages and because of a road traffic accident on the motorway there was no one available.

She called again the following night. The roaring and buzzing noises were even louder, she complained. But, by the time the police arrived only the sound of silence, unique to the countryside, could be heard. There was no evidence of bikers. No one else in the village had complained either.

"I'm not imagining this," she exclaimed when the sergeant suggested she could be charged with wasting police time if there were any further reports without evidence. Her reluctance to have anything to do with the villages had not endeared her to him.

The following night Greta decided to take the matter into her own hands. She set up a tape recorder. As soon as the bikers started up she would record the sounds. The police would have to do something then.

But there was nothing, not that night or the night following. She gave up, put the tape recorder away and settled down for a long rest. She wished she'd invited Michael over for a nightcap, the disturbed sleep and lying awake for the past three nights had her on edge. He would know how to relieve her tension and his wife was away, but of course he wouldn't be able to leave the children alone in the house. Odd that, the way Nessie had run off to take care of that old school friend whose health seemed to be a constant worry without at least taking the twins.

.oOo.

Stephen and Nessie hadn't left the hotel suite since they arrived forty eight hours ago. Nessie had loved him more in that time than he ever remembered being loved, she made everything he had been through worthwhile.

It was the end of the previous winter when Oscar had driven Nessie to the hospital in labour. Her husband had been busy at the stables and had not come back for lunch as he usually did. She had crawled out of the cottage on all fours, her son Andrew ran out in front of his car as he turned into the driveway and he had to brake hard to avoid hitting him. When he got out of the car to check on the boy he saw her lying by the gate to the cottage, bleeding badly. He picked her up and drove her as fast as he could to the cottage hospital, just in time for the twins to be delivered safely. Oscar sent the boy to find his father, but he never found out why her husband had not returned for lunch, or even noticed she was gone by the time he arrived back to tell him she was in the hospital. Andrew had looked sheepishly at him, as if he had a secret he couldn't tell.

The memory of that moment, when he had had to leave her in the hospital played out in his mind's eye, so much had happened since then.

"I hate to leave you," Stephen said, stroking the back of Nessie's hair, leaving her in the safety and bliss of their hotel room.

"We've waited for each other for this long, what's another few days?" She reached out her hand towards his face "So handsome."

"And before?" he smiled at her.

"Ah yes, before too. You were so brave, I couldn't have borne it."

"It was the only way. She would never have let us have any happiness."

“Are you sure we can’t leave things the way they are? We have enough don’t we?”

Stephen kissed her worried frown.

“We do, but this is about so much more than the money, and really she will be fine. You mustn’t worry, you’ll be safe here,” he said firmly.

He rose, hating the lie and regretting having to leave her warm soft body on the king size bed. He started to pack the attaché case.

“My flight is in two hours. Get some rest and, by tomorrow, this will all be over and I will be back. No more goodbyes. Everything is arranged for the children to stay with your mum for a bit.”

Nessie nodded. She felt peaceful; Stephen: she rolled the name around her tongue. She preferred it to Oscar. She felt safe with him; he was so trustworthy, not like Michael.

Stephen had booked the trunk call for 5pm in one of the booths off reception. Nessie had no idea of the arrangements and he wanted to protect her as much as possible.

“Well, did it work?”

“She called the police. They found nothing and it’s been quiet ever since. She’s really burned her bridges with the sergeant.” There was something about the way he said “burned her bridges” that made Stephen shudder. He knew then Chatham wasn’t just doing this for the money, or revenge, he enjoyed the prospect of a kill.

“And Michael?”

“Yes, she called him over for a service. His wife’s away but you probably already know that.”

Stephen smiled. Yes, he already knew that.

“I’ll transfer the next payment tomorrow when I arrive in London. Everything set?”

”Yes. All set” the voice assured him.

Stephen hung up the phone and made his way to the airport.

Greta had first talked to him about her dreams of owning a stables and running a small fruit growing business during their engagement; the land at Deepwater seemed to Oscar the perfect opportunity and location for him and his new bride to start off their married life together. He had been surprised when she didn't ask questions about his plans for them to have a home near his parents when he told her, but she was busy with their wedding and he was glad he could surprise her. Only the surprise had not gone over as well as he'd hoped.

As he parked the car, he could already tell she didn't like his design for their house. The surprise soured even further when she tore into him for having made one of the bedrooms into a nursery.

"Do you not get it?" she screamed at him as she ran out of the room.

Despite the rocky start Oscar made it his priority to make Greta happy. He appreciated she had a good head for business, so decided to give her the reins to build her dream without interfering, even though he would have preferred a more collaborative, domestic and intimate arrangement. It was through her business contacts she introduced him to Chatham.

Chatham was a businessman whose ties to the underworld were widely known but never spoken about. Oscar knew Chatham had government contracts and fingers in all sorts of pies he didn't want to know about. The opportunity to design some buildings for Chatham had enticed him and Oscar closed his eyes to the less savoury goings on in Chatham's building and business empire.

Oscar still hoped for children. They had not spoken about starting a family since the incident in the nursery. Greta's dreams and panic attacks had not helped; they were intimate on Greta's terms - she preferred to please him orally and he rarely spilled his sperm into his wife. It was just after New Year in 1960 when Oscar found the blister pack of pills in Greta's bathroom whilst he was looking for fresh soap. He knew immediately what they were, they had been all over the news. The miracle of modern science, freedom for women, said the headlines although how she had got them he couldn't fathom. They were not available on the NHS. Oscar put his head between his hands. He wanted to speak to her, but he couldn't face another tirade of abuse. That was that. They had a life together, a compatible marriage, not the one he'd hoped for, but it would do.

But in the spring of 1963 all that changed. He had turned a blind eye to Michael, and when he saw her with Chatham's son in law, he again turned a blind eye. He wasn't about to give Chatham any ammunition that could backfire and create who knows what sort of havoc the man was capable of causing.

Oscar was enjoying a quiet moment to himself on the terrace when a stray dog ran across the lawn to the vegetable beds and started digging. The gardens were looking well-ordered and ready for summer. Greta was out and Oscar didn't want her to come home and find them a mess. She had spread her precious fresh compost over them only that morning.

When he'd faced Greta with what he had found later she remonstrated against his accusations and finally laughed.

"It wasn't a baby, it was a foetus, less than six months. It just came away. Anyway, at my age, you think I want some damn brat to care for? Deal with it."

Oscar staggered out of the house and drove to the church to pray, to beg forgiveness for whatever he had done that had driven her to bury their unborn child without a word. How had he not known, seen she was pregnant and what were her plans? He didn't want to think the unthinkable, but the thoughts came anyway, swirling like a deep mist, entirely dissipating the love he had once felt for her. The pieces came together, the trips to London, the putrid smell of boiled herbs in the kitchen. His body was racked with pain. A deep burning in the pit of his stomach giving birth to an anger he had not known he was capable of feeling, it boiled over and petrified itself.

It was Nessie who found him alone, sitting outside the church. He was crying, he couldn't even pray the pain away.

"Oscar, can I help?" She had sat down next to him, not speaking, just waiting patiently as he strove to breathe through the tears.

Perhaps it was her kindness. After he poured out everything he had found that morning, the bloody blanket, which he first thought contained a dead animal, he told about what had been going on with Michael. He was shocked when she told him she already knew.

"Michael has always been a wanderer," she said. "But he always comes back and he loves Andrew and the twins."

"How can you not mind?"

"Well, you've known it's been going on," she shrugged. "I guess we're both a couple of mugs not to do something about it."

"It's not just Michael, she is seeing someone else as well."

"Who?" asked Nessie, clapping her hand over her mouth as soon as the word was out. "No, don't tell me, it's none of my business. Sorry."

"It's alright," he said, "Someone I work for, his son in law. He would not be at all thrilled if I told him about his daughter's husband cheating with my wife. There'd be hell to pay."

"Well hell for her maybe, Greta I mean, but not for you, surely?"

.oOo.

Heathrow was bustling, despite the lateness of the hour. There was the driver that Chatham had promised, holding a card with Stephen's name printed in large capital letters as he reached the passenger exit doors.

"Know where you're going?"

"Yes, sir. I have very precise instructions."

As the car purred through London towards Surrey, Stephen began his preparations. Finally, the end was in sight. The careful planning had paid off.

Michael was surprised to receive a phone call from the hospital. His wife was supposed to be in Northumbria, he couldn't figure out how she was involved in a local traffic accident.

"I'll come straight away," he told the caller on the end of the line.

He didn't see the motorbike, which roared up suddenly, from behind.

Hearing the sound of the motorbike from inside the house, Greta rushed downstairs. She stopped in her tracks, as a familiar voice came from the living room, it couldn't be.... . She turned around slowly.

"Hello Greta," he said again walking toward her.

His face was unrecognisable but that voice, that distinctive accent, those eyes, they were his.

"Oscar?"

"Well done, Greta. Perceptive as ever I see. Sorry that you were so upset about the codicil, that the house gets to remain. Oscar's cousin Stephen will be very happy living in it."

"You....? You evil bastard."

"Takes one to know one, Greta."

She deserves no pity he thought as he looked at her cold face. It wasn't fear he was seeing, perhaps if he had he would have changed his mind. But the only thing he saw in her was the will to survive. He knew then, she was capable of anything. There was no time for pause or debate. His execution of her was swift.

Oscar had much to reflect on as he travelled back to Heathrow. And as for Michael, well his 'disappearance' would spare Nessie a custody battle. Oscar smiled. The 'letter' Michael had left for her was very convincing, he was thankful that Chatham had thought out every detail. Now he had to trust that the man would keep his word. There would be no question that the home Oscar had designed would finally have the children it deserved. The twins would have a solid home to grow up in, just like he had. Nessie hadn't known the plan, she would never have agreed. As Chatham pointed out during their hypothetical discussion about how to commit the perfect murder, a loose tongue or a conscience was not a good option. Like any good design it was always better to keep things tidy.

Neighbours

"All the world's a stage, and all the men and women merely players: they have their exits and their entrances; and one man in his time plays many parts ..."

William Shakespeare

Neighbours

Anna grabbed her husband's arm trying to shield herself away from the flashing cameras as they both left the court.

"Come on Anna, flash us a smile," called out one of the photographers and the chant "Anna flash a smile," started up among the rest.

Brian hastened his pace, Anna tottering in her black high heels to keep up, stumbled. The size too small dark skirt and jacket she had worn for the hearing were hot as the fabric pulled in the sun, making her sweat. She felt dishevelled, discombobulated and, perhaps more importantly, hungry.

"Please Brian, wait up."

"We need to get away from this pack of rats," he snapped back at her. "Come on." The verdict was not a complete surprise. His Barrister had told him a custodial sentence was unlikely, but the two years suspended sentence and community service was, he felt, excessive. Pushing Anna into the waiting taxi, Brian turned around to look at the expectant pack of photographers and press.

"Leave us alone, there is no story and I will sue," he said, jabbing his finger in the air, wondering at the same time what he could possibly sue them for. Foot in mouth, as usual, he reprimanded himself. His pin-prick eyes and slight frame did not match the threat of his words and the negative retorts back were immediate. The press did not like Brian.

"But you didn't lose Brian" Anna tried to convince him as she shovelled a mouthful of scrambled eggs and avocado between her apple blossom pink lipsticked lips. Her size fourteen blouse, tight across her ample bosom, popped a button.

Anna had insisted on stopping at the greasy spoon as soon as the taxi was out of sight of the press pack. She was always hungry these days – ever since she'd stopped having sex with Mike and was back with Brian. It hadn't yet occurred to Anna there may be another reason for her hunger and the tight feeling in her breasts.

"F'ing two years Anna, two bleedin' years of having to mind my own and do some sort of charity work because you couldn't keep your legs closed. You can say goodbye to that 'gong' too. They don't hand them out to criminals."

Anna reached for the red plastic tomato containing ketchup, "That's not nice Brian, I thought we agreed that we were drawing a line under the past." The ketchup malfunctioned as she spoke and a splatter of the red sauce landed in a line under Brian's nose, like a small moustache. Anna giggled.

Brian swiped at the line, spreading the ketchup across his cheek as well as covering his finger. He did not look or feel like a winner. 'Bugger it,' he thought.

Anna had claimed that she had no idea Mike could see their pool and hot tub from his second home further up the Mountain. Mike had claimed that his view precluded the view of the Wilsons patio due to the overhang, but they both knew they were lying. It was part of the frisson that had drawn them into an affair - an affair that resulted in Brian's current conviction for assault.

.oOo.

Mike had moved to Bexhill in 2001. Five years later, at forty, he was even more well known for his appearances on television and foodie chat shows. His extravagant taste for exotic foods prepared with different spices, cooked outdoors had led to Mike's BBQ Party being screened worldwide. The show appealed to both men and women and drew in millions of viewers who, in turn, bought his books and followed him in gossip columns and the new social media. By early 2006, Mike was King of the world of foodies . He also wasn't short of women, but the girls who came and went, with as much frequency as pop tarts are eaten for breakfast in America, did not satisfy his quest for the perfect partner. Someone he could settle down with. Problem was he had no idea what a perfect partner might be like, after his marriage to his childhood sweetheart Morgan, failed. He had been single since Morgan had kicked him out. The partnership had not been perfect and neither had Mike. But he had learned the hard way. Morgan was still reaping the financial rewards of his fame - thanks to her clever solicitor and Mike being overcome by guilt. He had gone against his solicitors advice and agreed to too much. In his solicitors words, 'unconscionable robbery'.

Mike graduated from catering college in 1986. The catering course had been a means to an end, and Morgan had pushed him to get a qualification, any qualification, so they could get married. In 1992 Mike started working as a chef for a gastro pub chain that had started to win awards when the documentary crew turned up to film them pre-service. The timing couldn't have been more perfect for Mike. The networks and especially the BBC were moving to include more regional broadcasting and regional accents. Mike's natural presence on camera, prepping fish, describing how to manipulate the fleshy bits in a strong Manchurian accent, made him an overnight success. Not since Wilfred Pickles had the network received so much mail about accents. This time favourably. "Mike's cheeky double puns hit the spot!" claimed one national tabloid.

Morgan had used the headline against him on several occasions when he increasingly failed to hit her spot. After she found a pair of lacy undergarments in the back of their car, the humour of the double entendre failed her and she left, or rather she made Mike leave. Morgan changed the locks and the modest Victorian row house in a once unfashionable area of West London eventually afforded her a four bedroom house in Suffolk. Mike didn't really begrudge what Morgan had gained from him financially, but he did miss her forthrightness and down to earth humour.

Taking the advice of his accountant, that his career on the up, might not last after he hit his forties, Mike had invested in property in the UK and bought a villa in Spain. His house in Bexhill, which overlooked the beach had a large terrace.

It was perfect for filming outdoor barbecues, it also became a tax write off. As did his house in Barcelona, with its wide terrace, pool, views of the Catalonian mountains and, as it turned out, the Wilsons patio. Although Mike had tried to keep the locations a secret, his personality and sociability meant exposure, which in turn meant he had to invest heavily in security. So much for the tax write off he complained to Gerald, whose forbearance as Mike's accountant was exemplary, given the chaos Mike seemed to cause, especially when it came to indulging women.

"Mike, you can't claim women's clothing as a tax write off," Gerald had moaned when Mike handed him a wad of receipts from Harvey Nicols.

"But she was work related," Mike grinned.

Mike was feeling restless. They had completed all the filming for the pre-Christmas special and how to Barbecue your Turkey. They didn't usually film on a Saturday but the weather had been against them and they needed everything completed before post-production started on Monday. The film crew had left and it was now all down to post-production and studio work before the series launched in time for the autumn/winter schedule. It has all been stressful though - the beach walkers and his neighbours had looked askance when the eight-foot decorated Christmas Tree and climbing Santa had appeared on his terrace in mid-July. The flock of seagulls had almost wrecked the Christmas Eve salmon, king prawn and trout extravaganza when they flew in en masse to raid the platter of seafood, left alone only for a moment. Like pirates they devoured their unexpected fortune quickly. The runner, a young girl in her late teens, was covered in small blobs of white shite, as she waved her arms and yelled, failing in her effort to see them off.

"Help yourself to anything that fits in the guest bedroom," said Mike pointing towards a door at the top of the stairs. She would find an Aladdins cave of 'spares' for unexpected overnight layovers.

"Mike you are incorrigible," said the dresser as the awkward teenager came down in a brand new LuluLemon top.

Mike shrugged, laughing. "Yep," he said. "I can't help it if Bexhill is better stocked than your average Marks and Sparks knicker department."

"Bonking palace," said the cameraman, "that's what your house should be called. Never mind Nirvana."

"Came with the house when I bought it." Mike smiled. He was used to the joshing from his crew. Any attractive new PA listed on the call sheet was immediately warned not to think she might have a permanent position however much was promised before bedtime; but the smile didn't quite reach his eyes. King of the BBQ he might be, but, despite not waking up alone most Sundays, he felt lonely. The King was trapped in the castle. The runner had been too young, he had limits and preferred women with a bit more savvy and experience. The ones who didn't have a melt down, or tried to make a second date, when he ordered them a taxi, after serving an elegant eleven o'clock brunch. He liked the rest of Sunday to himself, papers, a walk and when he was home, evening prayers at the local C of E. The minister had been sworn to silence about his congregant. And, as Mike's appearance boosted the regular attendance at Compline by fifty percent, the minister was happy to oblige.

Hence, on this Saturday night, for once Mike was alone. He had left a message for a couple of old-timers, women who knew the score, but they had both been busy and not flattered by the last-minute invitation. Mike picked up the phone to Donna, his personal assistant. Donna was semi-retired from working at the BBC as a continuity supervisor. Her formidable and extremely organised no-nonsense approach suited him and he suited her. Well paid, she could work from home and stop the endless commute to sets at ungodly hours. Donna's other profession was author of historical bodice-rippers under the name Felicity Cummings. Mike had been as surprised as a Victorian virgin on her wedding night when he found out about the racey mind of the bespectacled grey-haired spinster. He had knocked a newly copied manuscript entitled 'Destiny's Ride' out of her hand as they collided entering and leaving the lift at Television Centre. Donna rarely worked outside the drama department but one of Mike's shows had been badly reviewed for its lack of continuity. Donna had been summoned to supervise a studio recording and Mike offered her a job working for him.

"We have a lot in common," he had said at the time, winking at Donna.

"Hi Donna can you get me on a flight out to Barcelona first thing? I'll take anything going, ideally first or club, but I'll make do if that's not available."

Donna was used to Mike's calls coming in at unusual times, but thought his voice sounded off.

"Are you alright?" she ventured, unused to dealing with feelings of actual people, unlike the characters who flooded her mind with their passions.

"Yeah, Donna, I'm okay, just need a few weeks out of dodge."

Fourteen hours later Mike was strapped into club class waiting for take-off. The flight was unusually full.

.oOo.

The Wilsons, who lived on the other side of Bexhill, were also heading to the airport.

"For f's sake Anna, how much bleeding luggage do you need for two weeks away?" moaned Brian as he stowed the fake Louis Vuitton into the boot of the taxi.

"You do know that saying 'F' is the same as if you actually said 'fuck', don't you?" retorted Anna, ignoring the remark about her luggage. Brian was being a mongoose this morning she decided. Mithering about this and that and the expense of the taxi. Well she deserved a bloody taxi, she resolved, her accent slipping to Liza Doolittle before the interference of (H) enry (H)iggins. They were doing well weren't they? Brian and his little army of fishermen. The new building had achieved what he had hoped for and Brian's fish had finally made it into Harrods. Anna had had to practise putting the H in front of the store name and, in her opinion, her pronunciation was now perfect BBC, all ready for the invite to the Queen's Garden Party. Anna was convinced Brian would get a gong, as she called it, in the following years honours list. It was the least she deserved, she reckoned, after putting up with the smell of fish everywhere since she had married Brian. It was mostly alright, except the odour of fish even seemed to get onto his boxers. When Anna tried to sweeten the smell with natural flora, the lavender stems she had placed strategically between the sheets resulted in a trip to A and E. Brian's expanded cock not due to the excitement of having Anna, but a rather nasty allergic reaction, had caused much mirth amongst the medical staff.

Mike looked at the brunette, sliding her ample bottom into the seat next to him. The slight framed man following her stowed her luggage in the overhead.

Damn it thought Mike, looking around to see if there were any single seats left. There were not. Several passengers, used to travelling cabin class, had been upgraded.

"Dew like the windoh seat then?" She asked Mike. Her voice was pure Essex on the one hand, but there were undertones, as if she was trying hard to sound posh. It took him a moment to transcribe dew into do you, the O of window being over pronounced instead of winder, which was probably closer to her authentic dialect.

Mike decided to play along, replying in his broadest Mancunian, which was clearly not what she was expecting.

"Hey, aren't you 'im off the telly? My Brian likes you, reckons you've revived the fish industry single 'anded with your barbeques and what not."

"Yeah, that's me, but keep it to yourself. I'm trying to get away for a bit of a break."

"Ooo, awright then. Cheers." Anna nodded, raising her glass and gulping the cheap bubbles the stewardess was handing out.

Mike smiled. She was a bit of a laugh he could tell. He looked across the aisle at Brian. It was an odd match, she was full on, glamorous in a tarty way, but the bespectacled, balding husband looked quite serious. Already had his nose buried in some paperwork, and they hadn't even taken off yet.

"What's yer old man do then?" Mike asked. He didn't really want to know but talking to her would pass the time.

"Fish," she said somewhat subdued. "He's in fish."

Mike wondered what being "in Fish" precisely meant. Seeing, in his mind's eye, a younger image of the man opposite in full fishing gear, surrounded by cod attracting the eye of this minx with his daily catch. It would have to be a big one. She clearly had a taste for finer things than her birth right entitled her to. Bit like himself, Mike thought.

By the time they landed in Barcelona, Mike knew more about Anna than he had intended. Born in Dagenham, she had left school at fifteen and started work with Ford as a machinist. Brian was on an apprenticeship in the accounts department. They had met at the Christmas Party, when Anna's date had got drunk and abandoned her in the car park to walk home alone. Brian had come to the rescue. He was from Brighton. Anna thought he was a better catch than anything Dagenham had to offer up, so she married him. And, as it turned out she had been right. Brian's head for numbers and spreadsheets had made him a small fortune after he bought a failing fishing fleet in Hastings. The owner had been glad to get it off his hands before going bankrupt, but Brian had seen the potential. He now owned five of the most profitable fishing fleets on the South Coast.

"But what I don't get," said Anna, somewhat inebriated by her third glass of bubbles and a large gin and tonic, is why he always smells of fish. She pronounced is "phisshhhh." "I mean, phissshhh don't live in those bloody ledgers he's always staring at."

Brian adhered to a management style of getting one's hands dirty. As soon as the boats came back he was there, with the men. He loved seeing their catches. Touching the precious commodity that would keep Anna in the style of living to which she had become accustomed. Anna couldn't understand it at all.

As the plane landed, the passengers ignoring the please remain seated pleas of the captain and stewards, made their way to the nearest exit. Mike saw Anna disappear behind her husband, teetering her way down the steps of the plane. He didn't expect to see her again.

Well rested and enjoying the view under the warm afternoon sun Mike stood on his balcony, overlooking the view of Barcelona and the beach of Sant Pol de Mar. He was surprised to see a small patio below him, with a pool. That must be new he thought, certainly he didn't remember seeing the patio last time he was over. He was about to turn away when the voluptuous figure of Anna in a gold bikini and high heels appeared and spread herself out on a lounger.

Despite her ample size, Anna was a stunner. A brunette Marilyn Monroe Mike considered as he studied her almost naked form. Anna rose slowly from the lounger, turning to face the sun. She untied the top of her bikini, revealing her marvellous breasts. Mike inhaled. They couldn't be real surely, they were so perky. He adjusted the lens of his binoculars and realised that Big Johnny had woken up and that his imagination, like Donna's was capable of full-on bikini ripping from a distance. He gasped as the premature ejaculation spilled out into his new white shorts.

"Oh my god," he said aloud, "how the hell did that happen."

"Signor?" Mike hastily put his hand over the wet patch as the elderly maid, who lived in the village, entered with the plate of fresh appetizers and a jug of sangria, he had asked for. Damn Tommy Hilfiger he thought, realising the appeal of the stretch fabric had not contained him.

As soon as the maid left Mike hurried back over to the edge of the patio, but Anna was gone, taking her magnificent breasts with her.

.oOo.

The Wilsons had purchased the sight two years earlier. It was an almost derelict villa, and the estate agent had long given up hope of making a sale. But the price was good and Brian saw the opportunity for an investment. It would need some money, but at the end of the day, the investment would be profitable. Anna wanted a villa, and as her husband, she saw it as his duty to provide one. In one way she was right, it was less expensive than constantly jetting all over the world, as some of their friends did.

The patio had been finished just two weeks before they arrived, it had been a work in progress since last summer and Anna, fed up with the constant delays, had insisted on giving the work to a different contractor before they left previously. Fed up with Brian trying to penny pinch, which had contributed to the delay, Anna managed the final negotiation herself, in a hotel room in the centre of Barcelona. Brian, blissfully unaware of the deception, had been self-congratulatory about his Spanish negotiating skills, and striking such a bargain.

Anna had spied the glint from the binoculars focused on the patio, almost as soon as she lay down on the sunlounger. She didn't know for sure that the patio belonged to Mike, but she had a good idea. Anna followed enough gossip columns to realise that they lived close by on the same mountain. She regretted choosing the gold bikini, that black swimsuit covered up the wobbly bits better, but it was too late to change now. She felt like a dancer in a burlesque peep show as she stood up and slowly unfastened the straps of the bikini, stroking the defined and perfect modelling of her breasts, thanks to the implants Brian had paid for. As she sat astride the sunlounger she was about to expose her freshly waxed brazilian when she noted the binoculars were gone and Brian had appeared. She'd have to take one for England. Thank god he didn't smell of fish she thought, as she acquiesced to his beckoning and followed him inside to the bedroom.

Mike couldn't sleep. He didn't know if it was the heat or the pent up frustration he felt about what he had seen. How was it even possible that a woman of her age, and figure, had set him off like that he wondered. Morgan had been skinny, light as a feather, she still was as the pictures that he surreptitiously looked at on her Facebook page showed. He didn't know why he did that, but it was harmless wasn't it? Anna was a full-figured woman, but she was all woman, he could see that. She was a woman who was fun. And fun had been missing.

Anna couldn't sleep either. Anna wondered if Brian was on some sort of self-improvement mission as he'd unusually had the appetite to take her several times, before and after dinner. Maybe he was having an affair and was trying to prove to himself that he was a good husband? But she quickly put the thought away. Brian would never have the initiative to take a mistress, and Anna was glad about that. Anna didn't regard her negotiations with tradespeople and the odd afternoon delight with a friend's husband as anything other than keeping herself in shape. How could she know she was still desirable and please Brian if she didn't take herself out for a test drive every now and again? Not having children had been a good decision, her weight was always a challenge and babies would have completely buggered things up. And she was a good auntie. The best Auntie, her nieces and nephews always said, as she showered them with treats and an abundance of the type of noisy battery operated gifts parents moan about.

The road to Mike's house was the only way up or down the mountain, so Mike realised that the patio he had seen the day before must belong to one of the smaller villas immediately below him on the turn. There had been a couple up for sale when he first bought his property. He smiled at the coincidence of meeting Anna on the plane. He couldn't get her out of his mind. He had other distractions already set up, but they weren't a challenge. He wondered if Anna would be. He doubted it, but her husband might be a problem.

Mike went out to the terrace to check on the patio. She was already in the pool swimming in a black one piece. No sign of the husband Mike noted, realising that throughout their conversation on the plane she had only ever referred to her husband as he. Mike fixed the lens of his binoculars on her speeding through the water, then turning to float, face up, making star positions with her arms and legs. She reminded him of a playful dolphin and he wanted her. The husband came out with breakfast on a tray.

'She's certainly got him well trained,' Mike thought as he watched the man set up the table with glasses, cutlery and napkins. He was wearing slightly too long baggy shorts, a white t-shirt with brown sandals and socks. "Poor bugger," Mike muttered, "she might help him out a bit with wardrobe."

The phone rang. It was Donna checking in to make sure everything was alright and to confirm that post-production had started well. "Everything looks great Mike, there's just a couple of sound issues, mostly because of those seagulls, but they said you could do that in a sound booth over there, and the recordings can be dropped in. How long are you staying?"

"Not sure yet Donna, but can you do something for me? I'd like to know about a business that's run out of Hastings. Fishing. Not sure of the bloke's name who owns it."

"Mike, there are lots of fishing businesses there, do you know anymore?"

"I think the same bloke owns a few fleets, I'll try and find out his name. Cheers Donna."

Minutes later an email from Donna pinged in. 'I think the one you're interested in is called Wilsons Fish Incorporated. It's owned by a man called Brian Wilson, he's bought five fleets over the last ten years and made quite a tidy sum.'

'You're a star Donna.' Mike typed his reply, whistling. So the husband was called Brian.

The distraction Mike had planned for the next couple of days was a woman called River. She was Canadian and has moved to Spain to marry a wealthy vintner. The marriage had not been a great success, but River had stayed, preferring the Mediterranean climate to the harsh winters Calgary offered. Perhaps it would be the perfect opportunity to throw a dinner party Mike thought, invite the new neighbours. Figure out if the challenge was worth it. He could take a walk, drop off a card with his phone number and see what happened. Now he had their name he had been able to figure out the exact location of the Wilsons Villa. He was impressed Brian being 'in fish' had clearly been a good investment. Villa's on this side of the mountain were not cheap.

"Brian, you'll never guess!" Anna almost flew at her husband who was pouring over spreadsheets at the indoor dining table.

Brian sighed. Whenever Anna sounded excited like that it usually meant he would be asked to spend money.

"We've been invited up the hill, to 'is 'ouse, the one from the telly I told you about from the plane."

Brian removed his glasses and stared up at her. She was still in the black bathing suit, glistening from the swim, her hair hung down her back, dripping onto the floor. He marvelled again at how he had managed to capture such a goddess. As a schoolboy and student he had failed at being able to get a girlfriend. Even Monica Jones had refused him a kiss and she snogged everyone for a cigarette behind the bike sheds. She had returned the whole packet of cigarettes back to Brian without a smile.

"Bit odd, don't you think?" said Brian. A perfect stranger inviting us to dinner all of a sudden.

"Oh Brian, he's not a stranger, I talked to him for the whole flight over."

His perception of her naivety struck him, it was charming. Anna always took people at face value. Generous to a fault, that was his wife.

"I'll say yes then. Alright with you?" asked Anna, picking up the phone. She had no intention of waiting for a reply.

The barbeque Mike prepared was effortless to him, but to Anna the feast was better than any of the stuffy restaurants Brian liked to take her to. Apart from Mike and River there were two other guests, also neighbours, who Mike seemed to know quite well.

"Do you speak Spanish Anna?" River had asked as she served her the champagne cocktail Mike had chosen, knowing Anna liked bubbles and would be impressed.

Anna giggled. "Oh no, sorry, hope you all speak English, I can just about order a croissant in French, I'm afraid. We didn't get no language lessons in Dagenham. Bottoms up," as she downed the glass. "This is lovely Mike. I love bubbles, me."

Mike almost spat his drink across the table, laughing. The other guests, both Spanish looked puzzled. They had visited England many times, but had never heard of Dagenham and Anna's English was very different to the conversational classes they attended in Barcelona.

As the darkness fell, when Anna looked over the balcony in the direction of her patio, she could just see the solar lights hung around the pool flickering. She had been right then, he had been peeking. Naughty boy.

"Good views from here," said Brian, coming out to join her.

"Yes, but clearly we are nice and sheltered, can't see us at all from here," she said pointing her finger away from the patio and hoping Brian did not look down.

"That's good," said Brian. "Don't want everyone getting an eye full of my beautiful wife sunbathing."

"No worries on that score," Mike said winking as he caught Anna's eye, "the overhangs keeps us all private."

"What are you looking at?" River said the next morning as she emerged from a deep sleep. Both the master bedroom and the living room opened out onto the patio and Mike was peering avidly through his binoculars.

"Just bird watching," he said casually, as Anna repeated her swimming regime from the previous morning, with Brian bringing out breakfast.

"Yeah, right," River said, her Canadian drawl hitting the note of ironic sarcasm which had attracted Mike to her when they first met.

"That poor sucker hasn't a chance with you around my horny little friend."

"Who?" asked Mike innocently.

"Brian. You're clearly gagging for it with his wife."

"River!"

"Well, honey, it was very obvious, sorry to rain on your parade and all. And as for the can't see your patio from here rubbish. It was just a good job he's so short-sighted."

"Ah, it's just a bit of fun, I doubt ...." Mike paused. He realised that this was an odd conversation to be having with the woman he had just made love to all night and who was staying over for a few more days.

"I don't doubt that you will Mike, but just be careful. Brian is really in love with her, and she might be a player, but he'll get really badly hurt."

"Right," said Mike. "Let's change the subject." Rivers' words were getting under his skin. She was right. Brian was clearly a nice man, besotted with Anna. But Mike couldn't help himself. He was used to getting what he wanted and what he wanted for good or for bad was Anna.

When Brian opened his computer, three days later, he was shocked by an urgent email from his finance director telling him to return to Hastings immediately. All the Wilson fleet was banned from fishing and the company was being investigated for drug trafficking. What the devil! That was why his phone was pinging all night.

"Anna, we are going to have to go home. There's a police investigation. They turned up late yesterday with all sorts of warrants and stuff. I'm needed for an interview. They think the business is a cover for drug trafficking."

"What! Well that's all rubbish Brian, you'll easily get it sorted. Fly over, do the interview and come back. You of all people. Drugs, they must be barking."

"It might take days, weeks to sort this out," said Brian.

"Well, if it does, then I'll follow you. Seems a shame to just pack up everything when we've only just arrived and the fridge and freezer stocked with all that delicious food. It is rubbish Brian, isn't it?" Anna suddenly wondered, they were rather rich for fish.

"Of course it is rubbish Anna. I would never do anything like that, you know that."

"You're as honest as the day is long" said Anna reaching down to give him a kiss on the cheek. "You'll see. Some tosser has made an error and you'll make them pay for the inconvenience. I'll get an overnight bag ready for you." Anna bobbed her head up and down, trying to convince Brian he had nothing to worry about, and should head off without her.

Mike watched as the patio remained empty and Anna did not appear for her morning swim. River had left the night before. They'd had quite the row after she found out what he'd done.

"How could you Mike? Honestly, people do make money in fish."

"Not that much," said Mike. "Not honestly anyway."

It was about eleven o'clock when Mike took a walk down the mountain road and saw Brian with a small bag climbing into a taxi, without Anna. He dropped the note he'd written earlier through the door, inviting both Anna and Brian up to his house for cocktails at six pm. Anna saw him through the glass door and was about to call, come in, when she saw the paper fall onto the mat.

"Hello Anna, no Brian? Said Mike as Anna rang the bell at ten minutes after 6pm. She had worried about being too early or too late, and she thought she had remembered an article in Cosmo that ten minutes was polite lateness, whereas twenty was not. She had selected a pale green chiffon cocktail dress. The dress was rather old fashioned but it suited her figure and she didn't want to give the wrong impression, after all the invitation had included Brian. How was Mike to know he was away? The black halter neck, the red satin and the low cut lavender maxi with thigh length slits lay in a heap on the floor of the bedroom.

Mike had set out a bottle of Champagne and three glasses with canapes near the faux log fire. The evening mountain air was somewhat chilly for the time of year.

Anna's eyes started to water as she explained why Brian wasn't with her. She wasn't really pretending to be upset, but perhaps seeming more upset was appropriate she thought as Mike put a sympathetic arm around her shoulders, and removed the silk wrap.

"You poor woman, that's terrible news. You should have phoned and cancelled. I honestly would have understood, or maybe there's something I can do to help?" Mike's words were smooth, reassuring, and measured in his response.

"Thank you. You're very kind. I must look like a terrible mess."

"You look lovely, come and sit, a glass of champagne will help."

"Oooh, more bubbles, you're right, bubbles always make things better."

Just who seduced who that evening is a question neither Anna or Mike could answer honestly. As he slid his hand inside the green chiffon, Anna's hand began to caress his already erect penis. Five minutes later they were both in his bedroom, naked as the day they were born.

"Oooh that was luverly," said Anna, reaching for the glass of champagne she had not managed to finish.

Mike ran his hand up and down her back, watching her breasts in the mirror on the opposite wall as she drank. They were magnificent, not real, but magnificent all the same. He wanted to bury his face in them and blow bubbles. As she said, bubbles always make things better. Her curvaceous body and enthusiasm for sex had satisfied him more than he could have imagined. How Brian kept up Mike had no idea.

He was exhausted, physically. Mike's only complaint was that intellectually Anna was not much of a challenge, she was naturally funny. But the the saying, "lights on and no ones home", occurred to him more than once

Brian's interview with the police in Hastings was, as Anna had predicted, short. The Pavlovian response to the unsubstantiated claim by a local grass had got the chief into hot water and Brian was back on a plane less than twenty four hours after he had left. He was going to call Anna, but he arrived at the airport late and had to run to the gate which was about to close. He tried to call her as soon as he landed but there was no reply. Well, not surprising he thought, Anna was not an early riser or she was already out in the pool.

Brian was puzzled by the heap of clothing on the bedroom floor. Brian held the gift of duty free perfume he had bought on the plane behind him, to surprise her with, but the bed was made. It was unlike him to be spontaneous with gifts, but she had been so right about the outcome, he wanted to do something to show her just how much she was loved and appreciated.

"Anna, where are you my love?" he called out, as he made his way through to the patio. His face fell when he saw the note from Mike, inviting them both for cocktails the night before, on the table. Anna's mobile phone with it. He froze, the box of perfume slipped from his hand and crashed to the floor.

"Brian," Anna gasped as she arrived home several hours later. She was wearing a white linen sundress Brian had not seen before. Brian was sitting at the dining table, head bent as usual, over figures.

Brian had resolved not to ask her outright where she had been when she came home. He already knew the answer. His mind had gone round in circles from thinking the unthinkable to rationalising why Anna might have stayed at Mike's. After all the villa was very remote, perhaps she had been too afraid to sleep here by herself.

Anna came close and bent over to kiss his cheek. "Hiya husband, I knew you'd get it sorted," she said brightly.

"Oh Brian, is this for me?" Not noticing Brian's expression, Anna picked up the box of Channel from the table.

"How was Mike?"

"Mike?" Anna flushed as Brian handed her the note. "Oh Mike, yes, he was very kind. I went up there for a drink, as you see, he invited both of us, and, well we chatted, and it got so late, he let me use the spare room. He was worried about you and wanted to see if there was anything he could do."

"That was nice of him." Brian's voice was flat.

"Oh Brian, you're not being a silly billy are you, thinking that I've been a naughty puppy?"

Brian swallowed. His throat was dry. He didn't want to believe that at all. But suddenly he was back to being twelve and Monica Jones handing him back the pack of cigarettes.

Anna crouched down to meet his face with hers. "I wouldn't Brian, you know I wouldn't."

Anna's call to Mike was short and sweet, "Brian's home, I'll be on the patio at five o clock. Sorry, can't come back up to yours tonight." she whispered.

Mike rolled his eyes. It was too late to make other arrangements now. Whatever she thought she was going to do on the patio would not make up for the disappointment.

"Didn't quite work mate" said Mike a few minutes later, into his phone. "Yeah, well thanks for trying. I'll be in touch."

Her performance was worthy of an Oscar, Mike thought as Anna, appeared on her patio, dead on five. She wore the long lilac gown, with slits to the top of her thigh. She carried a white scarf and had piled her long hair up on her head. There was no sign of Brian. Anna put her index finger into her mouth and sucked in her cheeks as she inserted the finger in and out, slowly. Her other hand stroking her breasts, pushing one and then the other forward. Mike was mesmerized. Big Johnny was already pushing at his shorts as she gyrated her hips. Turning, she pulled up the back of the dress with the scarf, running it from back to front revealing her naked butt. Mike was in agony and just about to finish himself off when Brian appeared, carrying a jug of what looked like Sangria and two glasses.

"Noooo," the words slipped out of Mike's mouth involuntarily as Johnny retreated.

What was she doing, a peep show for him and Brian at the same time? Slapper he thought ungenerously.

"Sorry Mike," I thought he was asleep, she said later when he finally picked up his phone. She had called three times.

"Did you like it?" she asked. "I've been going to burlesque classes, they're really fun, all the rage."

"Yeah, you're good, but god when Brian appeared, well ..."

"I know dahlin, but just think I can perform another time, that's something to look forward to."

"Can you perform up here, in person? I'm desperate to see you, touch you."

"Only if Brian's not around, and that's unlikely. Sorry."

Mike thought hard after he hung up. Plan A didn't work, but perhaps Plan B would. She might not be the brightest bunny on the planet, but he had to have her again. It was riskier, well for Brian anyway, but it would give Mike the time he needed to sate himself. Burying his face in those magnificent breasts, until he was ready for her to go back to Brian.

When the Spanish police arrived at the Wilsons Villa two days later, Brian was taken away in handcuffs. A new report had been handed into the British Police and in accordance with EU laws in the matter of dealing with drug traffickers the Barcelona Police had acted swiftly.

"Oh my God, poor Brian," wailed Anna into Mike's chest.

"Look, it's probably all still just a big mistake," said Mike calmly, stroking her back and pulling her closer until her breasts were hard against him.

"But ...."

"Ssshhhh, my love, I will help," said Mike positioning himself next to her and reclining them both onto the capacious sofa as he kissed her.

Mike's Plan B, had gone better than Plan A. Brian was returned to Hastings for questioning and Anna, grateful to Mike for his help, had obliged by staying at the villa, even though Brian was released, pending further investigation. Three more weeks went by and still his wife was not by his side.

Mike convinced Anna she was better off waiting in Spain, until all the fuss blew over. He made her no promises, and to be fair, she didn't ask for any. She seemed to accept they were lovers, but he had no idea what she was thinking about for the long term. It was hard to figure out what she was thinking much of the time, apart from sex and performing burlesque for him, which she thought she might turn into a career.

"I just can't come back until this is all over Brian," she had told him when he called. All our friends, my family have told me, I am better off here, while, you are in all the papers there. I know you did nothing wrong, but no-one else seems to believe you."

The papers, as Anna indicated, had caught wind of the story, but so far no one had wondered about Anna, or why Brian had been in Spain. Anna hadn't spoken to her friends in the UK or her family, she was simply following Mike's reasoning, but Brian didn't need to know about that she thought. And, Brian's arrest and subsequent troubles probably would have died on page two if it hadn't been for a fan of Mike, sharing a picture on Facebook. Mike had taken Anna into Barcelona for a shopping spree when the photo of them, sharing a cocktail and a not so discreet kiss on the rooftop terrace of the Hotel San Pedro, was taken.

An eagle eyed freelance photo reporter had spotted the picture and flown out to Spain. He hung around Mike's villa. He was experienced enough to avoid the security guard and using a long lens to get the images he wanted. The following Sunday the image of a smiling Anna, with Mike's hands cupping both her breasts from behind was plastered all over the Tabloids. The headlines were full of double entendres about Mikes ability to handle flesh and suggesting Anna had a lot to flash a smile about.

Brian was devastated. The ongoing investigation was fruitless, the searches of his house, the boats, his office and computers had come up with nothing. Yet, he felt like a total failure, back to Monica Jones he muttered, when the police finally closed the investigation. The bevy of reporters that were constantly on his doorstep, did not help. Brian wondered how he could possibly go on, now that he had lost Anna to Mike.

But Anna's conscience was troubling her. The newspaper picture of Brian, with his head bowed, standing outside his now closed offices, touched her.

"Oh Mike, I think I should go back and see him, poor chump."

"Yeah Anna, perhaps you should," said Mike. The photo of him with Anna had shocked him. He liked publicity but what was being written, connecting Brian's recent woes to Anna and Mike's affair was bringing the chickens a little too close to home. If anyone put the threads together, he could find himself in trouble.

"I think I should go back too. There's the sound stuff to sort out and post-production might need a couple of hand-held retakes. Those seagulls have a lot to answer for," he said. Mike was trying to keep it light but the affair was over. Anna had been fun, but he was ready to move on. He had not spent almost a month with the same woman since Morgan. Plan B had gone further than he'd intended. Brian's business was all but ruined according to the Daily Mail.

.oOo.

"Hello Brian." Anna hadn't told Brian she was on her way back and was shocked at his appearance. He looked grey, his normally respectable indoor shirt and cardigan hung off him, as did his trousers. The already thin man had lost pounds. "Oh Brian, I'm so sorry." Anna clapped her arms around him. Brian did not resist or reciprocate, it was as if she were hugging a statue.

The two shady characters waiting for Mike in Bexhill when he let himself in later on Sunday scared him. What use was all the security he was paying for if photographers and anyone could let themselves in and do what they wanted. These two were really bad news though. He knew if he tried to run they would get him. He put his hands up to his face, protectively.

"Look," he said, "Sorry if I stirred up trouble. I didn't mean to ruin things for you guys. I didn't even know there'd been a bust until I got back this morning and saw the local paper. I don't know what Geordie was thinking".

"Yeah, well it did. The whole route was almost wrecked thanks to you. You're lucky we talked his nibs out of what he had planned for you when you showed up. What was it all about anyway?"

"Nothing really," said Mike. "I got carried away, thought I had found the woman of my dreams, but she wasn't."

"You did all that, took all that risk for a bit of arse?"

"Yeah, stupid or what."

The taller man shook his head in disbelief. "More than stupid. You'd better watch it, or you'll never have an arse again," he said "and now you owe. Right mate, got it?". As if to drive home the point he took one of Mike's knives from its block and drove it into the wooden chopping board. "Got it?"

Mike was ashen. He nodded fervently. "Got it." His voice, a whisper, as he struggled for breath.

As soon as they left Mike poured himself a large whisky and flopped onto his bed. He had messed up royally, but, hopefully, it was over. Although what he now owed, and when he would have to make good, he dreaded to think. He looked at his watch, and decided to go to Compline. He needed solace and calming down, the final prayer service of the day, asking for a safe journey through the night, seemed fitting . He had risked everything and for what?

He arrived at the church early. The only person present as he sat at the front of the pews. He picked up an order of service left over from the morning. The title was Forgiveness and the printed reading from Samuel 2, was the story of David and Bathsheba.

1 In the spring, at the time when kings go off to war, David sent Joab out with the king's men and the whole Israelite army. They destroyed the Ammonites and besieged Rabbah. But David remained in Jerusalem.

2 One evening David got up from his bed and walked around on the roof of the palace. From the roof he saw a woman bathing. The woman was very beautiful,

3 and David sent someone to find out about her. The man said, "She is Bathsheba, the daughter of Eliam and the wife of Uriah the Hittite."

4 Then David sent messengers to get her. She came to him, and he slept with her. (Now she was purifying herself from her monthly uncleanness.) Then she went back home.

Mike stopped reading, he remembered what happened next. David had arranged for Bathsheba's husband to be killed. Mike had arranged for Anna's husband to be arrested and in doing so had ruined him. Not much difference thought Mike, thanking God that Anna, unlike Bathseba, was not also pregnant as a result.

"Hello Mike, it's good to see you," said the minister, holding out his hand. Mike swallowed. Was he imagining that this man, wearing the robes of faith, could see what an absolute bastard he had become.

Mike knew what he had to do. The talk with the old reverend had been clear. If he was going to move on, put things right within himself, he needed to own up and ask for forgiveness. Mike was surprised by how relaxed the old man had been as he described what he had done. But then, given the stories and the antics of the men that God had forgiven, if the bible had any truth to it, he had certainly read about worse. Maybe he had even heard worse. Mike didn't know.

Mike made his way to the Wilson's Bexhill house. It was late, but he didn't want to wait until morning in case his courage failed him overnight.

"Who the hell's that at this time of night?" Brian's voice could be heard through the open window, Mike guessed was the bathroom.

"Mike, what are you doing here?" Anna's face was clearly shocked seeing him stand there. "It's late and well, it's not really a good idea. Brian's getting ready for bed, so am I." She held tightly onto the door, trying to make sure he didn't try and enter.

She didn't look well, pale. Mike thought.

Mike could see Brian making his way down the stairs behind Anna. He was carrying a wrench.

"Brian, let's talk mate," Mike held up his hands, palms open. " I've not come here to fight."

Whoosh, the sound of the wrench swinging at Mikes head was followed by a crack as it hit Mike's skull.

Anna screamed, "Stop it!" and tried to get between them. A neighbour, hearing her scream, called out they were calling the police.

Brian dropped the wrench, as Mike fell to the floor.

Anna repeated Mike's name over and over, kneeling over him, she was quite bloody by the time the police and ambulance arrived. Brian had reverted to a statue. His by now familiarity with handcuffs and being escorted into a police car evoked no sound or protest as the uniformed officer led him away.

.oOo.

"Wow you really did it this time," said Morgan, scrutinising the bandage circling Mike's head.

Mike smiled ruefully. "Thanks for coming."

"What are ex wives for?"

"Only wife," replied Mike, making a grab for her hand.

Mike had not wanted to press charges against Brian, but the assault was deemed too serious to let it pass. Hence Brian's appearance at court on September 22nd 2006.

The Christmas barbeque party special brought in more viewers than the networks could have hoped for, proving that no publicity was bad publicity. Mike, having had a big bang on the head, was brought to his senses. He proposed to Morgan on the anniversary of their divorce, ten years earlier and made a plan to settle down and be faithful to his, almost perfect, happy ever after partner.

It was mid October when Anna found out she was expecting. As usual, without words for feelings, accepting whatever situation came along, she merely looked surprised when the doctor told her the results of the examination.

"So I'll miss the show then?" she said

"Sorry? The show?" The doctor was puzzled. It wasn't the usual response from a patient on finding out they were, at least, three months pregnant.

"Burlesque. Been practicing all year. You should go, it's lots of fun. My Brian loves me performing for him."

"I'll bear it in mind," said the doctor.

"Well I'm sure Brian will be thrilled," said Anna, rubbing her belly. Their lives had changed so much since Barcelona. They had had to downsize and sell the villa, but Brian seemed to have managed to rebuild the business. Anna was content enough, but a baby, and just whose baby, was a conundrum she had not expected.

"One thing Doc," she said as she turned to leave the consulting room. "How might one know the exact date that this all happened?" She pointed to her belly.

"Date of the last period, measurements, how the baby develops, we'll know more precisely after the scan as your recollection of dates are a bit vague."

"Right" said Anna. "Thank you."

Anna's route home took her passed Mike's beach front house. Brian had relocated them to the South side of Bexhill, into a new development of new slightly smaller executive builds. He had wanted to move closer to the business, further out of town, but Anna liked being able to walk to the local shops. Brian hadn't realised the new home meant he was in the same neighbourhood as Mike, and Anna had chosen not to tell him.

"Better to let sleeping dogs lie," she said to herself aloud, as she passed Mike's House. Wondering exactly which night and by whom the tiny life growing inside of her had been seeded.

The Herbalist

"The truth is, no one of us can be free until everybody is free."

Maya Angelou

The Herbalist

On June 1st 1967 the driver of the blue roadster wished he had taken the ring road home to Daybridge, 14 miles north of Tollcross on the coast of Fife. He sat motionless, his hands covering his eyes, trying not to look at the lifeless body of the woman and her bicycle that had flown over his car, landing with a crude dense thud on the road. The back wheel of her bicycle clicked, as it continued to spin around. He hadn't felt any impact between him and the cyclist, a tragic conundrum.

The entry to Tollcross often took motorists who were unfamiliar with the winding lanes, by surprise. A historical clock tower divided the road into two around the green with little warning. In recent years accidents and deaths of animals and humans had declined thanks to the ring road diverting through traffic away from the small town. Whilst this solution had saved lives, it was bittersweet for the shopkeepers who had lost casual passing trade.

Jo's gallery and gift store faced the green. She had been putting the finishing touches to the new summer window display, when she saw the horrible accident. Maggie's body and bicycle flying over the car and landing on the green. Panic rose up inside her, Jo's heart was beating fast as she screamed and ran over to where Maggie lay.

"Maggie, Maggie.... ." she cried out, frantically, as she lifted the limp hand to feel for a pulse. Finding none, she tried her neck, desperate for a sign of life. Blood was seeping from the back of Maggie's head. In her heart Jo knew it was hopeless, but she couldn't bear it. Maggie, her lover, her lifelong partner, couldn't be dead. "Help her please, help her someone.... ."

A group of Tourists who had arrived moments after the accident slowly filled the road. Someone called instructions to phone for an Ambulance and the Police amongst the hushed murmurs and gasps.

"Has anyone checked on the driver?" One of the tourists said.

As the words were spoken a woman screamed. Jo looked up to see The Reverend Thaddeus Beauchamp silently falling from the church bell tower. His body landed in a bloody mess in the church grounds, on the opposite side of the green. The tourist group groaned together in shock and disbelief.

Jo, still holding Maggie, screamed. Her body collapsed onto the ground, as she fought for breath, next to Maggie.

Jo felt a strong hand on her shoulder, pulling her up. It belonged to Tony, who owned the cafe next to her shop. She looked up at the kindly face of her friend, her eyes flooded with tears. He knelt down, held her close, trying to comfort her.

"Come away Jo." His voice was calm, despite his own devastation caused by the death of a woman he too loved. The police had arrived, moving everyone away. Jo didn't want to leave Maggie. It took both Tony and a police officer to help her into a chair in Tony's café, where the tourist group had been asked to wait.

Having settled Jo, Tony offered the group of tourists and their driver cups of tea, coffee or lemon water to alleviate the shock of the double tragedy that had marred the beautiful sunlit morning. The ambulance crew and police went about their gruesome tasks, removing the bodies. The police wanted statements from everyone.

As the cafe finally emptied and the tourists, police and paramedics departed, Jo sat on the stone steps of the clock tower, staring at the green where Maggie and Thaddeus had both laid dead. Her whole body was shaking as she sobbed inconsolably. Tony covered her in a bright striped blanket and tried to tempt her to sip from the glass of hot chocolate sitting next to her, until she was ready to talk.

"He was responsible for her death."

"Who Jo?"

"Beauchamp," her voice contorted, the word sharp and harsh. Tony patted her on the shoulder. He wasn't surprised by what she said, although he couldn't see how it could possibly be true. The things that Thaddeus had done and said to Maggie before he'd gone on holiday were vile, but how could he have possibly caused this.

"Thaddeus? But, despite what we all thought, the man's dead for God's sake, this has to have just been a horrible accident Jo. Two horrible accidents."

Jo looked down, squeezing her hands together for comfort. Spoken aloud, she knew she sounded ridiculous. After all she had seen the man falling from the bell tower. But Tony had been away and didn't know about Maggie's meeting with Thaddeus and the manuscript. From what Maggie had told her, Thaddeus's own story was horrible. Neither Maggie nor she could have imagined what had contributed to the fear the man had about Maggie's practice. And Maggie had found out everything, revealed his secrets. Surely that had to have prompted him to take his revenge? Despite what Maggie had said, that she had met the real Thaddeus, that he was 'frail and vulnerable'. Frail and vulnerable people were not exempt from doing terrible things thought Jo.

"Thanks for the chocolate Tony. I'm going home, I need to be alone."

"Call me if you change your mind. I'll come by in the morning anyway."

Jo nodded, she managed a half smile, her face felt frozen. She couldn't get the images and the events of the morning out of her mind.

Jo had overheard the driver talking to the police. His upturned face tear stained, blotchy and tormented. His voice had been rapid as he blurted out: "Damn it, I know this road, I was born near here. I didn't hit her. I swear I didn't."

The words haunted Jo. They didn't make sense, but he was right, it was almost as if Maggie's bike had taken flight, over the car. There was no clear damage to the bike and there wasn't a scratch on the car. Maggie would have easily seen the roadster coming.

As the car and Maggie's bike were prepared to be taken away for further examination, Jo had asked if the bike could be returned to her. She had no legal claim, she was not legally Maggie's next of kin. The policewomen touched Jo's shoulder as she spoke.

"Come to the station and make a request. You never know her family might like a close friend to have it. It's not damaged at all from what I've seen."

But Jo knew she would be the last person the family would want to have anything of Maggie's. Everything will be packed and taken away or destroyed. There would be nothing of Maggie left for her. Margaret Dunbar senior would make sure of that. Jo ran over to the flat above Maggie's shop. At least, she could save Maggie's research from being trashed she thought as she stuffed the stack of papers and books into a box.

The following morning Jo woke up with a jolt from a nightmare. The cheers of the crowd as Maggie, wearing medieval clothing, was thrown into a loch, echoing through her head. She was sweating profusely. Facing herself in the dresser mirror Jo flicked the cows lick from her fringe to the side. "Bedhead," Maggie would have said and helped her brush the thick unruly blonde hair. The dresser was littered with Maggie's brushes, pots and perfumes. The bedroom had been a sanctuary for their lovemaking, hidden from the prying and unsympathetic eyes of the world.

Jo had met Maggie ten years earlier, while waiting for a plane. The swinging sixties may had been a time of free love for heterosexuals but at least ninety percent of the population in Great Britain regarded same sex couples as being sick, needing treatment. In 1957 the church had a stronghold over the morals of the many. Male homosexuality was still a crime in Scotland, but few publicly thought women practiced this sinful abomination. Thus, Maggie and Jo conducted their partnership with as much secrecy as they could, maintaining separate homes, and allowing the rumours of lost fiancée's and broken hearts to be spread without challenge. The only person who understood the exact nature of their relationship was Tony. And their relationship had been complex. Jo's confidence had often bothered Maggie. Maggie's hesitation, lack of belief in herself and her capabilities had driven Jo mad. Maggie's mother had tried her best to intervene, but she had eventually given up, or rather her failing health had left her with less energy for bullying Maggie.

How could she face today, Jo wondered as she pulled on the Chinese silk robe Maggie had given her for Christmas. But she knew she had to keep pushing herself forward and made her way slowly down to the kitchen.

The normally neat kitchen table was covered with the papers and books she had collected from Maggie's flat. It was going to take a month of Sundays to sort out Maggie's chaotic system Jo thought. There were still so many unanswered questions. Jo felt her spine tingle as she poured boiling water into the cafetière they had brought back from France, another reminder of their partnership. Maggie was everywhere, in everything Jo touched, looked at or even wore. Jo scrunched the silk as if she were trying to find the life of the giver inside the fabric.

.oOo.

Maggie Dunbar was born in Chester le Street in 1932. She was the late child of Margaret and Henry Dunbar, whose infant sons had both been lost due to an outbreak of cholera in 1925. Growing up Maggie was happiest when she was with her father, mixing and experimenting with liquids and natural flora to create potions. Foraging in the woods or gazing at the sky through his telescope learning about the constellations, dreaming about what life forms might exist on other planets. From Primary school to Junior and finally High School her ambition to be a scientist never wavered. Perhaps it was her mother's depression about the loss of her baby sons that caused the relationship with Maggie to flounder. Her never-ending worry that Maggie too might die was stifling for both Maggie and her Father and, in the end, they both left.

Maggie relentlessly pursued a place at Edinburgh University. As a female she knew she had to do better than any of the male candidates and worked hard. Her father was proud and told her he would be there for anything she needed or wanted, even though he was leaving her mother. Maggie's mother wanted wedding bells and the promise of grandchildren and she resented her daughter's refusal to comply with her wishes. When Maggie graduated with honours in Medical Science in 1953, Margaret Dunbar refused to attend the graduation, but Henry came. It was the last time she saw her father before he died the following year. Maggie was offered work in a new company with headquarters in Belgium. Her work took her around the world and finally to British Columbia where she and Jo met, waiting for a plane.

The two women were instantly drawn to each other, in that rare way that happens when two like-minded souls meet. Maggie recognised in Jo the quality of her creativity and intelligence and Jo in Maggie the power of passion for her work in alternative medicine. They contrasted each other physically, Jo, tall blonde and angular, Maggie red haired and shorter, with an hourglass figure that was a constant battle to maintain.

Jo had been travelling across North America and Alaska, combining a holiday with business, finding artwork and gems to make into jewellery to sell in her store and capturing images to paint. British Columbia was her last stop before heading back to Scotland.

When they realised they were travelling the same route, Vancouver to the East Coast and then across the Atlantic they requested to change seats and sit next to each other for the long journey to London. Jo planned to get an overnight train to Scotland, Maggie was staying in London to visit the Apothecary Gardens before going to see her Mother in Durham and then back to Edinburgh, to complete a Ph.D.

"Small world," said Maggie as she and Jo clinked glasses of gin, waiting for the final take off. The delays, bad weather and turbulence would normally have had the confident Jo white knuckled clutching the seat throughout the flight. But, listening to Maggie, exchanging life stories with each other, took her mind off everything.

In the taxi they shared to travel into London Maggie told Jo the other reason she had avoided being persuaded into marriage. Jo leaned in to kiss her, her touch igniting the unspoken attraction and passion they both felt.

The room at the Station Hotel had been a spontaneous decision for them both. But the following morning Maggie was agitated, she pushed Jo away as she tried to comfort her. Post coital dysphoria and Catholic guilt had her in its grip.

"Maggie, I remember the first time I was loved too. It's okay. You told me you were scared. It's the way we are, it's not wrong."

She had looked at Jo, her green eyes blank.

"I'm going to hell for sure now," she had whispered, getting up from the bed.

But hell or not, following the visit to her mother, when Maggie arrived back in Scotland, she'd called Jo.

"I'm sorry," said Maggie when Jo answered. It had taken her all day to pluck up enough courage to make the call. She had berated herself endlessly for the way she and Jo had parted and she had convinced herself of certain rejection if she called.

Jo recognised her voice immediately. "No need to be sorry, I have been waiting for you to call, on tenterhooks," Jo's voice was excited, but reassuring. "Let's see where this goes, I can't wait to see you again."

They spent the next couple of years travelling back and forth between Tollcross and Edinburgh as they got to know each other. Accepting their differences, drawn closer by the values they each shared. Their mutual love of wildlife, classical and jazz music and contemporary art. Both wary of the potential for harm to either of them if their relationship came under public scrutiny. The first time Maggie visited Tollcross Jo invited Tony to dinner. Tony knew immediately that the women were lovers, but then he too had a secret that would expose him to harm and the cruel discrimination of the law. Tony's family had disowned him when they realised he would never marry or become a priest. As the first son from a Catholic patriarchal heritage his obvious sexual inclination was an embarrassment. Tony had won over the haters in the Village by his generous and kindly nature. When Maggie finally moved to Tollcross in 1962 the three of them often joked they were a statistical anomaly for a town the size of Tollcross.

Once she completed her Ph.D. Maggie had plans to open a complementary holistic herbal medicine centre. When the shop opposite Jo's with a flat above became vacant, it seemed like the obvious location. As Maggie prepared for her opening, the curtained windows and unusual signage sparked local curiosity. The opening event was a huge success.

Tony galvanised support and goodwill amongst the locals and created an herb infused fruit punch to mark the occasion. By the end of her first week Maggie's appointment book was almost full. The shop was beautiful. Together Jo and Maggie had sourced and repainted some classic style furniture to show off the oils and herbal remedies for sale.

The night before the event Jo gave Maggie the canvas she had secretly painted for her. Maggie gasped when she unwrapped it, it was stunning. One of the best pieces Jo had ever painted, the standing stones at Calanais under an iridescent milky white sky.

It was under a sky such as this, on a visit to the Isle of Lewis two years earlier, that they made their vows to each other.

"I want to marry you," Jo had said, taking Maggie's hands in hers.

"So let's," Maggie replied. "I can't think of a more perfect place and setting."

"Tomorrow? Here, our own vows?"

"Yes, witnessed by Mother Nature and Father Time."

They spent the following day collecting flowers and writing their pledges to each other. As the sunset and the night sky became bedazzled with the sparkling stars of the Milky Way, they stood facing each other in front of the stones and vowed to love each other until death. They both chose words that were oddly traditional, but the spirit of the moment was more blessed to them both than any formal Christian or civil wedding, had they been allowed.

The one flaw in Maggie's happiness that marred the opening was the ongoing feud with her mother. Her mother was neither physically or emotionally well, and it was hard to forgive the spiteful and cruel things she did or said about Maggie. The letter she wrote to Maggie after the visit with Jo was vile. Yet, despite everything, Maggie didn't want to give up on a relationship with her family and invited her mother, aunt and both cousins to the opening.

"They're not coming Jo."

Maggie held out the one-page letter written on the familiar blue Basildon Bond her mother used to write her short monthly missive full of complaints. The tidy tight black writing representing the closed and dour personality of the writer.

Jo hugged her, enveloping her body. Jo, almost five feet ten. Maggie, just under five foot.

"Enough," said Jo. If your mother cannot accept you the way you are, then perhaps it's time to move on."

Jo felt herself lucky to have been blessed with a more distant family relationship. Her mother had certainly not understood her daughter but she had allowed her the freedom to grow into herself, unlike Maggie's mother. Her mother had been proud of Jo when she opened her shop, in 1950. The world was changing, rations were still in play but people were starting to shop for nice things again. Jo's gifts as an artist and designer were timely, inspiring for a world emerging from fear and scarcity.

Over the next years Maggie and Jo's businesses flourished. Their relationship, the friendship with Tony and the acceptance of the locals gave all three of them a sense of inclusion and wellbeing they had not found within their families.

But, in 1965, sparked by the arrival of the new Rector, Reverend Thaddeus Beauchamp, something darker evolved that divided the populations of Tollcross and Daybridge. The outgoing Reverend Philip Madden had been a kind and gentle soul. His love of animals and birds was evident in his unorthodox annual 'blessing of the animals' service. Word had spread and the church was always mobbed with animal lovers, bringing wild and domestic animals for the blessing in June on the Sunday closest to the Solstice.

Maggie and Father Philip, spent time together discussing different herbal and natural treatments that historically had been the provenance of some of the early religious orders. His compassion and openness to others beliefs and understanding made him popular amongst the laity and he had a strong following of admirers from believers and non-believers alike. He helped Maggie release some of the guilt she felt about her strained and broken relationship with her mother and the resulting shame and guilt that still intruded on her relationship with Jo.

Before his move to Tollcross, Thaddeus Beauchamp had served for three years as a curate and came with a reputation for ambition and a stricter more evangelical theology than that of his predecessor. The first sign that he was unafraid to rock the boat was to cancel the 'blessing of the animals' service and publicly denounce rituals and practices founded within what he described as pagan worship and other Anglo-Catholic idolatry and traditions.

In September 1965, Maggie won a coveted international award for leadership in alternative therapies and complementary medicine, the local paper celebrated her publicly and Tony threw a party in her honour. It was a week later when a carefully printed tiny brown envelope arrived in the post.

The crude letters stuck onto the white writing paper, "Witches are an abomination, sayeth The Lord" cut out of a newspaper was, in Maggie's opinion, right out of an Agatha Christie plot. The words hurt but her mother had said worse. It was the second letter that was more disturbing," Exodus 22:18 "Thou shalt not suffer a witch to live. BE WARNED." The capital letters of the final statement made Maggie shudder and she was visibly shaking when Tony arrived with the daily morning cappuccino he regularly brought her.

"Time for a break and a blether? What's the matter Maggie?"

"It's this, its horrible nonsense, but it's ruined my day so far. Who would send something so vile?"

"Do you think your mother is behind it?"

"No, I checked the postmark, it was posted in Edinburgh, the other one was posted in Aberdeen. And she's frankly capable of writing worse than this, has written worse, so has my aunt."

"The other one?" Tony looked puzzled.

"It just said 'witches are an abomination'. This one feels more menacing, threatening somehow."

"Do you want to report it to the police? They might be able to track whoever the sender is."

Maggie shrugged. She didn't want to tell anyone about the letters, somehow the words brought back the feelings she had of disappointing her mother by her pursuit of science. Her sense of being different from the other girls.

"Tony, please don't tell Jo. I don't like having secrets between us but this is a really busy time for her - the run up to Christmas, getting everything ready and orders starting to arrive. I can't think there would be anything the police could or would do either. I'll talk to Jo if this keeps happening, or I can't manage it. Please Tony, keep this to yourself for now."

Tony nodded, he wasn't comfortable about keeping the secret from Jo but he agreed, it was Maggie's story to tell when she was ready to, and she was probably right about the police, given his own experience after a nasty assault.

The letters continued, Maggie kept them filed away, telling no one, not even Tony.

A week before Christmas Maggie returned from a trip to see her mother. It had not gone well, but at least she had tried. Maggie burst into Jo's store, excited to see her. Jo was exhausted with local Christmas shoppers and last minute requests. Seeing Maggie she held out her arms. Forgetting their normal discretion, they were in full embrace and a long lingering kiss when the door was flung open by Reverend Thaddeus Beauchamp.

The three of them stood in awkward silence for a moment.

Jo was about to speak when the rector threw up his arms, palms stretched out in front of him.

"Two bitches and a witch, I should have known, the tide of evil darkness is a cloud wherever you go." His hooded eyes penetrated Maggie. He swung his arms down, and pointed at Jo.

"It's not too late for you to be washed in the blood of the lamb. Save yourself." Turning on his heel, he swept out of the shop.

"Oh God," exclaimed Maggie. "Of all the people to......" her voice trailed off as she looked at Jo.

"He'll tell everyone, the whole village will know."

"Oh Maggie, everyone has known forever, they just haven't said anything. Lesbians don't exist in places like this. We're just a couple of odd ball spinsters. They prefer not to think about what we might get up to." Jo spoke calmly. Her logical confidence trying to reassure Maggie.

"But now," Maggie whispered, "that man, that man who is supposed to do good and help people find love, will stir up hate. It's who he is, it's what he does."

"What on earth do you mean?"

"Let's lock up here and I'll show you. I haven't wanted to tell you and last week I discovered, well I finally discovered who was behind the letters. My suspicions were right."

"Maggie, you're not making any sense, what haven't you told me? What letters? What did you discover?"

"Come on, I'll show you".

Jo locked up and they made their way to Maggie's flat. Maggie pulled out the pile of envelopes each containing a sheet of white writing paper with cut out printed words that were glued on in random patterns. 'Witch' said one. 'Evildoer', another. 'You will burn in Hell, Satan's mistress.' 'Your time will come, I am watching you.' 'He is watching you and waiting.' 'Beware you are not wanted here.' 'Leave or die.' There were several others using different words to denigrate Maggie and her work as an herbalist.

Jo looked in disbelief at the stack of vindictive and spiteful papers. The one she had received was insignificant by comparison.

"For goodness sake Maggie, how long has it been since this started. Why on earth did you not tell me?"

"Four months, they started after the award. I became suspicious Thaddeus was behind them when a client told me Thaddeus had handed her a tract about the evils of disobeying God's word and consulting with a witch. Me. When she described the look he'd given her, well I just shuddered."

"About a week later some of my clients started to cancel their appointments or dropped in to say they did not need their next prescription. You remember I had five or so workshops at local schools cancel? I had been invited to be the speaker at the WI in Daybridge, they cancelled. Two months earlier they were all very interested in the local history and how herbs have been a part of the way of life here for hundreds of years." Maggie paused.

"I'm sorry Maggie, I should have paid more attention to how things have been for you. Just with the run up to Christmas and getting everything ready, well you know. I was in the studio, then in the shop, really we only saw each other for about four hours a week over the past few months. I've really let you down." Jo's words tumbled out. "We should report these to the police."

Maggie shook her head vigorously.

"I didn't want to stir up any more trouble. I wasn't one hundred percent sure it was Thaddeus writing this crap until last week. I saw him post the envelope with my own eyes when I was in Daybridge. It was almost as if he wanted me to see him. But of course he had no idea about us then."

"He didn't know, but, Maggie, he did send me a letter too. Warning me not to be friends with you. I wished I had told you. But honestly, what sort of creep does this. A coward, is what he is. But cowards can be dangerous. Are you sure he's not worth bothering about, reporting?"

The two women hugged each other, trying to ease the pain they both felt by the magnitude of hatred and prejudice being levelled at Maggie.

Maggie poured them both a whisky. "Cheers."

"I love you Maggie, I can't bear someone trying to cause you pain." Jo held Maggie tight as she spoke, nuzzled into her neck.

After they made love, Maggie determined not to allow Thaddeus Beauchamp or anyone to spoil things.

"Jo, you are right. This is wrong, he isn't going to ruin things, we simply won't let him. I for one am not going to take anything he does or says seriously. Let him try his worst and be damned by me, the witch!" Her laugh, infecting Jo with her lightness.

But, Maggie was right about the influence Thaddeus would try to have. Over the next few weeks even though after Christmas was a slow season, local trade at Jo's gallery dropped dramatically. Whilst no one said anything directly to her, when she was out and about, she felt a coolness in the welcome when running for messages in the village store, or in the pub. Other dog walkers seemed to hurry on by when she was walking Shep. Tony, who also received a letter warning him to stay away from the women for the sake of his soul, remained their closest friend. His business was less affected, but even he noticed the lovely warm cafe, with its delicious coffees and home-made food was no longer frequented by the followers of Thaddeus.

Maggie decided to burn the letters, rather than take the matter to the police. She hoped by doing nothing, things would calm down, return to normal.

Jo and Maggie became used to being shunned but managed to carry on with their businesses thanks to tourism and clients from Daybridge, out with the church, and some new clients from the housing development.

Since Maggie moved to Tollcross a development of social houses, built by the local council, had brought new families to the village. Some of the newcomers, the ones who went to church and tried to fit in with village life were made to feel welcome, but the others, the ones who did not attend church or who were from other cultures and religions were given the cold shoulder. Some of the families got on with things, others asked to be moved, realizing their new location was not an ideal worth pursuing given the prejudices they experienced.

The Askham family were one of the last to move in. Emily Askham was a widow with three small children under ten. Her husband had been killed in a workplace accident and Emily found herself starting life again. Angus, Alastair and Jennie were quiet well-mannered children who quickly integrated into village life. Emily was a kind woman and the older residents took to offering help with child minding and baking treats for the children. Emily felt that she had suddenly gained a huge family full of mothers and grandmothers. Rev Beauchamp made a point of including Emily and her children into Church activities and she found herself on various rotas for cleaning, flower arranging and baking. Although Emily had been a regular church goer before, she found some of the Reverends beliefs a little strange and hard to accept, but she was too afraid to say so.

One day, five year old Jennie had a febrile seizure with a fever and chickenpox. Emily was beside herself with worry, despite being reassured by the hospital staff that this was something that could be managed and would be unlikely to occur again.

Emily had no car and no telephone and could not easily get help if a seizure was to occur and none of the neighbours were home. Emily remembered that she had seen Maggie's sign for herbal and alternative therapy in the village and she decided to drop in, after walking the children to school.

Maggie welcomed Emily and advised her that a warm bath with some mustard Raye seeds can bring down a fever and help prevent a seizure. Maggie also stated the importance of seeking medical help if a seizure did occur. Despite being busy and run off her feet by the additional demands of her own mother, whose failing health made frequent visits necessary, Maggie also offered to help Emily with the boys if she needed to take Jennie to hospital.

They were in the middle of this conversation when the door burst open and Thaddeus Beauchamp, in a black cloak held up a silver cross and screamed, "Witch."

He began jabbing his finger in mid-air, pointing towards Emily.

"Bring not you or your children here under her spell Madam. She will soon meet her maker, her time is up. I will rid this place as my brethren did before me of this evil doing."

With a dramatic wave of his hand he turned and left as suddenly as he had come.

Instead of the tactic sending both women down on their knees in fear of their lives, Maggie collapsed in a heap of laughter, but Emily looked as if she was about to faint.

"Honestly," Maggie said later as she described the scene to Jo and Tony, "he looked and sounded like a bad actor in a Hammer Horror, I think he's completely lost the plot."

"Hmm, well I think you should stay on your guard," said Tony. "I don't trust him not to do something completely bizarre. That was a very public statement."

"I didn't know whether to laugh or cry. The whole thing was so ridiculous. But poor Emily did refuse to take the parcel I had done up for her."

Jo looked at Tony, she too was worried that Maggie wasn't taking Beauchamp's behaviour seriously enough.

"Maggie, it really sounds like he was threatening you. Maybe we shouldn't have burned those horrible letters. I think you should report him."

"Ah he's just full of hot air, a bumbling hypocrite. I'm sure what he did today would get him into deep water with his higher ups. Perhaps I should report his behaviour to them.

Tony nodded. "Well, that at least would be something."

Jo agreed.

"Okay, I'm still in touch with Father Philip, I'll ask him for some advice."

As Maggie wrote to her old friend she reflected how much her life had changed. She was no longer the lone focused scientist, she was free, happy content with her lot, and would be more so if she could fathom exactly why it was that Thaddeus Beauchamp was so intent on making her an enemy rather than living and letting live. If his purpose as a priest was to convert people to his belief he had an odd way of going about it. Surely, he didn't really believe she was in a pact with the devil whoever the devil was, pondered Maggie, secure in her agnosticism. So far neither Presbyterianism, Catholicism nor the belief of her learned Professor, a Hindu, had convinced her of any particular order of deity. Father Phillip was the closest she had come to seeing positive faith in action.

The letter she received back from Father Phillip surprised her. He agreed that there were some things about Thaddeus that were odd, especially his fixation on anything he thought to be connected to the dark arts, such as herbalism. But, Father Phillip emphasized, Thaddeus was a harmless and devout Christian. His use of scripture to frighten Maggie was likely intended to convert her, misguided as the action might seem. His suggestion to Maggie was to let it ride itself out. Be the bigger person. Try and talk to the man. Be forgiving. He almost begged Maggie to let the matter drop. He himself was not feeling well, his age was beginning to slow him down and he regretted not being able to meet.

"This is not what I expected at all," said Maggie to Jo after they both finished reading the letter. "It's almost as if he thinks I'm in the wrong for how I have reacted."

"Well, if you remember Father Phillip was always on the fence about wrongdoing and punishment. His work with the local young offenders and the prison was very liberal, according to the parole officer who lives in Daybridge. There was a falling out of some sort which is why Father Phillip gave up his work as chaplain to the young offenders. This was before you moved here."

Maggie looked thoughtful, "I have no idea what to do now."

But Maggie's brain was in process, the rational brain that led her into science told her something was off about the way Father Phillip had responded.

"Police?" offered Jo.

"No, something more practical. I am going to talk to the Moderator."

"Wow," said Jo, "Right to the top then?"

"Not exactly, I know the current moderator from years ago, he was quite a lowly figure back then, I think he'll remember me. In the meantime I am going to take some of Father Phillips advice and try to talk with the Reverend Beauchamp."

"Are you sure?"

"Yes, I have to. This situation, this hold we feel he has over us, and this division he has created in the town - it can't go on. I have to do something."

"WE have to do something," said Jo, putting her arms around Maggie.

Maggie reached out to the Moderator and to some other local officials she had met through her Ph.D. She thought they might be able to help her piece together what motivated Thaddeus in his zeal against herbalism. What she found out had nothing to do with herbalism. By the end of her research, as she methodically wrote her findings about his life story Maggie began to feel deeply sorry for the man who had demonised her.

It was the end of May when Maggie decided she had to talk to Thaddeus. When she told Jo that she was going to meet with him alone later that evening, Jo was worried.

"Please let me come."

"I can't Jo, some of this," she pointed at the manuscript she had written, "This is too personal, it wouldn't be fair on him to talk about what I have found out with you there."

"Alright, if you insist," said Jo, "but if you aren't back by ten, I'm coming over to the rectory, I'll bring Tony. He should be back from his trip by then." Tony had been away for almost a month in Italy.

"Fair enough Jo, but I will be fine. It's Thaddeus you should feel sorry for, despite everything."

"So, Father Phillip was right?"

Maggie didn't say anything. She could feel her jaw tighten and bit her lips.

"Maggie? Father Phillip?" Jo questioned, puzzled.

"I'll tell you, in good time, but first I need to talk to Thaddeus."

It was a bright evening. The promise of long light on the eve of summer, with an unusually warm wind off the sea. She had baked some biscuits, bought a bottle of sherry and some lemonade. She had no idea if Thaddeus drank, and even if alcohol was appropriate for the discussion she wanted to have with him. She just knew she didn't want to go empty handed.

Thaddeus held himself stiffly as he answered the door. He seemed unsure about whether to let her in or not before he beckoned Maggie to enter. The hallway was dim, lit only by a table lamp. He looked outside and then shut the door quickly as if he was worried that someone might have seen her.

"Thaddeus, I want you to know I have not come here for any sort of argument." Maggie blurted the statement out, as she removed her papers from the bag and handed him the remaining contents. The action changed his demeanor, his body softened and looked her in the eye, nodding. He led her into the drawing room which was sparsely furnished, and very changed from when Maggie used to visit Father Phillip.

The bookshelves were full, almost overflowing with different theological texts, bibles and history.

"You have made more space for yourself. It was so full before, when Father Phillip lived here."

"Why do you call him Father Phillip, he is not Catholic?"

"Yes, I know, it's what he called himself." Maggie was unfooted by the question. She wanted to avoid any sort of disagreement, no matter how small, she had meant her observation as a compliment.

"What are those?" Thaddeus was pointing to the set of papers Maggie held in her hand.

"It's the reason I wanted to talk to you, to see if I could help you see that I am not like .... Like, your past."

"My past." His face tightened. "I have no idea what you are referring to, and as for what you do, well I have been warned to leave you alone, so if that's all you wanted to ask me, then you might as well go. Stop wasting both your time and mine."

"Warned?"

"Father Phillip. You asked him to intervene, and that's what he did. I am unlikely to be staying here now."

"I don't understand, Father Phillip almost admonished me for asking him about you, saying you were a very devout Christian."

"As I am."

"Can I have a few minutes, please? I'd really like to talk to you."

Thaddcus hesitated, the atmosphere in the room heavy with his concentration as he considered her request.

"As you wish. I am a Christian, as you stated, it would be churlish to refuse a member of my parish, and I have been firmly reminded that you are a member of my parish." He indicated a large green armchair that had seen better days on the opposite corner of the fireplace.

"Thank you."

Maggie did not know how to begin. Her research had led her down a dark path and she was worried how he would take what she had found out about his past.

"Well?" said Thaddeus.

"You are very against my profession, and I think I understand why. I just hoped we could talk about how very different what I do is from what you experienced at Cornton School.

Thaddeus turned as pale as a ghost. "How do you know I was at Cornton? Those records were sealed."

"Yes, the names of the pupils are sealed but Cornton was one of the places I studied in my Ph.D., the misuse of plants and experimental treatments that cause significant harm, even death and possibly countless suicides. What they did at Cornton, to boys as young as eight, giving them hallucinogenics, the sexual abuse, it was the pure evil you accused me of, and no wonder. You thought I might be just like them. Father Phillip, or, as he was then, Phillip Baxter, a young teacher, just out of college. You knew he and I were friends. But Thaddeus, I had no idea about his past."

"You need to leave, please, leave now." Thaddeus stood, unsteady on his feet, his breathing was shallow and Maggie recognised that he was in the midst of a panic attack.

"Breathe, just breathe and it will pass. Alright, I will go, but you need to know that this can't stay hidden forever. The extent of the abuse has to be told. It wasn't just the misuse of herbs and concoctions that was going on."

"How did you find out so much?" his voice was almost a whisper.

"I found another victim. He's given me a lot of information which I plan to take to the police. I wondered if you wanted to make a statement too. Put the ghosts of the past behind you?"

"No, I don't want anyone to know. Please, leave it be."

"For all we know, the people involved in Cornton are still abusing boys in other organisations. They have to be stopped."

"But they're all old now, and some are dead. Look at Phillip, he's over seventy."

"You feel compassion for him?" Maggie was curious.

"No, not compassion. You wouldn't understand. No one can understand what happens to a child when their innocence is taken from them by someone you are supposed to trust."

Maggie stared at Thaddeus, closing her eyes and putting the pieces together, the animal services, the children's camps, the welcoming of young families. All designed to give him free and easy access to young children, innocents.

"Is that what's in there?" Thaddeus pointed to Maggie's papers.

"Yes. Everything that I have found out so far, dates, people, the statement from the other victim, even some photographs."

"You've been very thorough."

"I had to be sure, I know that the police will have to investigate, but I needed enough for them to take it seriously. There are some important people involved in the cover up."

"Can I see it, will you give me tonight to read it and think about what I want to do?"

Maggie hesitated. She hadn't had a chance to write out a second copy, but she still had all the research at her flat, and the notes.

"Yes, of course," said Maggie finally. "I'll come for it tomorrow. I'm getting a train into Edinburgh in the morning"

"Well?" said Jo as Maggie made her way upstairs to the flat.

"I'll tell you all tomorrow Jo, after I've delivered the manuscript to the police in Edinburgh. But what I will say is, it's Thaddeus who is the victim, his behaviour is driven by fear."

"Okay, if you say so. Bursting into your shop as he did does not make any sense to me. Why Edinburgh?"

"There's too much at risk if I share it locally, I think. Did you know anything about Cornton?"

"Oh? The place where they sent delinquent children and made them mad?"

"Something like that."

"No, although a friend of my cousins went there I think. He was quite a head case when he came out."

"He would be," said Maggie. "What I have found out about the place, what they did there was worse than what my mother would call 'Hell' I think. Certainly, hell on earth for the children who were sent there. This may not all be over for a while, but when it is, do you think you and I could go somewhere, celebrate our vows. We didn't really have a honeymoon, and this research, well it's been harrowing."

"I know," said Jo. "I think going away is just what we need. Let me think of a place and surprise you my darling."

Maggie held out her hand and the two women made their way to Maggie's bedroom.

"Sleepover at mine tonight?"

For the first time in weeks they both felt a sense of relief. That the cloud of malice was finally passing, heralding a renewed equilibrium.

Maggie roused Jo from a deep slumber with a breakfast treat of French toast, with a generous amount of maple syrup and scrambled eggs. She had wanted to get an early train into Edinburgh, but they had slept in. Maggie was nervous, wondering how exactly turning up at the police station with her manuscript would go. Would they take her seriously even?

"Are you sure about this Maggie? I can come with you." Jo's voice was deep, her early morning voice Maggie called it.

"You have a ton of work today, you already told me, finishing the new windows you've put so much work into for summer and you're already late for opening. I'll be fine and home mid-afternoon I imagine. I want to pop into a couple of shops after the police station." Maggie dressed carefully, casual enough for the bike ride to the station but professional enough, she hoped, for the police.

"Thaddeus, are you there?" Maggie called through the letterbox of the rectory. She was going to be late for the eleven o'clock train if she didn't get a move on. She ran over to the church to find it was still locked, which was unusual.

Turning back to the rectory she was surprised to see Father Phillip shutting the front door and heading away from the church. Maggie called out to him but he didn't turn around, did she imagine that he was quickening his pace she wondered?

"I know what you did," she yelled, surprising herself by the spontaneous outburst, triggered by anger.

Maggie hesitated, confused about whether to still go to Edinburgh without the manuscript. She went back to the flat to gather some of her notes. Looking out of her window she saw Father Philip slip inside the clock tower. Damn him. She left the notes on the table, she could easily put together another manuscript if needed, and they could take her statement and follow up with the evidence. It was backwards, but something urged her, her heart was thumping, she had to report it all, today. Grabbing her bicycle Maggie started to ride purposefully toward the clock tower, heading for the station.

.oOo.

Jo was still slumped on the floor of the kitchen when Tony arrived. "I have news," he told her.

Jo shook her head "I can't bear any more bad news and I can't think you could have any good news."

"It's true," he said, I don't have any good news, but I do know what happened. Why Maggie was killed."

"She was killed then, it was him, that bastard."

"No Jo, it wasn't Thaddeus. It was Father Phillip who killed her, he killed Thaddeus too and someone else, in Livingston. I don't know the connection. Phillip was arrested this morning, it was on the early news. I guessed you hadn't heard."

"But why? I can't believe it."

"I'm guessing the answer lies in that mess of papers you have. Apparently, Father Phillip broke into Maggie's flat in the early hours of this morning. That's how he was arrested. One of the stragglers leaving the pub saw something suspicious and called the police."

"It's to do with Cornton," said Jo. "That school where they did all sorts of experimental tests on children, Maggie didn't tell me what she found out, she was going to do that after she had spoken to the police."

Tony made fresh coffee and they started to read through Maggie's notes. It was grim reading, a systemic pattern of sexual, physical and emotional abuse. The abuse had carried on for over twenty years. Orphaned children, and children from poor and disadvantaged backgrounds lives had been ruined. They had all suffered hugely and in some cases had become perpetrators themselves. Like Father Philip. Thaddeus

Beauchamp, real name Anthony Bowgett born 1937 in Glasgow. Parents deceased 1941. There was also a signed statement by a man named Roger Curlew from Livingston.

"I'm guessing Thaddeus's parents died in the Clydebank bombing," said Jo. "Maybe they both worked there. No wonder Maggie ended up feeling sorry for Thaddeus."

"I can't believe the evil that a so-called government organisation perpetuated and covered up when they found out what was going on," said Tony.

"I can," said Jo, "look what happens to people like us."

"True," said Tony, "here, in Italy and the good old U S of A."

"I think it's everywhere," said Jo. Her face, wet with tears.

.oOo.

The inquest into Maggie's death found that she had been killed by a pellet gun and trip wire. The pellet had been fired at her head, the trip wire was strategically placed, and it could have hurt anyone. How Father Philip had known he would be able to target Maggie remained a mystery. No one other than Maggie had seen the furtive figure enter the clock tower, or noticed as he walked back to the church, using the old vennel, as a short cut. According to the pathologist the shot was taken with precision and expert timing. The driver of the roadster was called to give evidence. He had been through a wretched time since thinking he might have killed Maggie.

As for Thaddeus it seemed he had been dead for at least twelve hours before his fall from the church bell tower, pushed over the turret by Father Phillip. He had been poisoned.

"Father Phillip is not as frail as he looks," said Tony as he and Jo left the hearing. "How on earth did he get Thaddeus up to the top of the bell tower?"

"Maybe he had help," said Jo.

"Oh let's not get all Miss Marpley, Jo."

Jo nodded. It was too tragic to be light-hearted. She had lost the love of her life, the biting cold hand of grief had her firmly in its grip, and the plans she had for her future in tatters.

“We have each other,” said Tony, “I know it’s not the same, but we are still family, right?”

“Most definitely Tony,” said Jo, as they walked arm in arm, away from the court.

“Did she do the right thing do you think?” Jo asked Tony later as they settled together in her flat, looking through the photographs of Maggie, whose life was cut too short.

“Her research, exposing Cornton and all those people at the top who knew what was going on do you mean?”

“Yes. Absolutely. It’s just tragic that it cost her her life.”

“It seems speaking up often does,” said Jo. She was unaware then that her words were not only historically true, but an accurate forecast of things to come. As men and women, speaking up against injustice, for diversity and inclusion, would have their lives taken from them as Maggie, her soulmate, had.

Sweet Dreams

"What we have once enjoyed deeply
we can never lose. All that we love
deeply becomes a part of us."

Helen Keller

Sweet Dreams

"I'm so sorry for your loss, Harry." He looked at the woman speaking to him through a mask. Her voice jogged him back to the present. She told him she had sat with his wife, Brenda, until the end. She looked kind enough, but he should have been there, not this stranger. Except to Brenda, his Bren, he already was a stranger. She had died without him. The last thing he had wanted. Hc had begged, pleaded to be allowed to wear whatever contraption or layers of plastic were needed to sit with her in the last days, but the refusal had been firm. No exceptions. Everyone was very sorry.

He knew he had lost her that day on the beach. He went to fetch them both an ice-cream, almost two years before she died. By the time he came back she had wandered away from the old wooden bench. The one they always shared whenever they visited. He looked around, worried. She wasn't far, just standing by the old pier, tapping on a wooden pole. Tapping it like a woodpecker with her fingers, instead of a beak, rhythmically.

"Bren, what are you doing?" Harry said as the ice creams began to melt, the creamy consistency running down the cornets onto his fingers. He handed her one of the ninety nines. "Come on eat up, or it'll run away."

Bren had laughed, that tinkling bell like laugh he had first heard in the pub, all those years ago. It was deeper, but still there.

"Run away," she said. Her eyes gave a hint that those words still meant something. "Run away, we ran away," she repeated, becoming more excited.

He nodded, taking her arm and pulling her into him he guided her back to the bench.

"Yes, Bren, that we did my darling, that we did." He patted her arm as they ate their cornets in silence and thought about the first night he had set eyes on her. Travelling down the lane of memories they each held of their 75 years together. His were clear, hers less so, like tendrils of mist they came and went.

The pub had been dark and noisy when Harry arrived. As he pushed his way to the bar, tripping awkwardly over someone's foot he almost knocked the glass of beer out of her hand.

"Sorry," he had said absently.

"Two left feet is it?" Bren had retorted, winking at her friend. She was wearing a lilac dress with tiny white flowers. He was still in Naval uniform. He had no idea then that the petite brunette was an Air Transport Auxiliar (ATA) pilot who flew some of the biggest planes from one side of the country to the other. Doing her part for the war effort. She had teased him later when he presumed she was a 'girly' girl.

They had thought that nothing of what they saw during those war years could be worse, but it turned out they were wrong. Bren's illness, her dementia, had robbed them of so much during the last five years of their lives together. Her empty mind reminded him of the street of houses where their friends had lived, a decimated cavity where once life and laughter had been.

There had been very few moments of lucidity over the past months. An occasional memory, triggered by a smell, or a word or a touch. Or one of the stories he read to her. Or when they listened to music. But that day on the beach was the last real day they had spent together, as husband and wife, as Bren and Harry, before she went to live somewhere else. He cursed himself again for making the choice to have her move in to the care home, where he could not be with her. Would she have made that choice if it had been the other way around? He had driven himself mad with second guessing.

The decision was made after she had wandered away one night. She had walked for miles in her nightdress and slippers. He and Roger had found her freezing cold at the edge of the canal, sitting on the grass. She was singing, one of the old songs. One of the songs they used to sing together.

"Dad, you can't go on like this." His son Roger had been angry about being woken up in the middle of the night to help Harry look for her. "Susan and I have talked about it, Mum needs to be somewhere where there are trained people who can look after her. None of us are getting any younger."

Harry, aged ninety five was still upright, shrewd, optimistic and thankful for every moment he had. Roger, at sixty nine seemed to Harry like a grumpy old man.

Roger and Susan, their beloved children had turned out well enough, but they led busy lives filled with consumerism and holidays abroad. There was little time left for their parents or, it often seemed to Harry, their own children and new grandchild. Bren had been thrilled when she learned she was going to be a great grandma. It was a cruel twist of fate that as the pregnancy came to term, her illness meant she had little capacity to know her own granddaughter, let alone who the new baby was.

Of course, none of them could have seen that a pandemic would make the care home a prison for Bren.

For over seventy years Bren and Harry had only been parted for the two remaining years of the war. They ran away to get married in 1943, two days after they met. They kept their nuptials secret until 1945. Neither of their families would have objected to their match, but organising a wedding and getting permissions would have taken too much time. Harry was due back from leave. They hadn't once regretted the spontaneous decision, or the lack of formal celebrations, although Brenda's mother insisted on a double family gathering as soon as she knew they were married. She begged and borrowed everything, camouflaging the tiny cake in paper and card to resemble three tiers, covered with tissue flowers and painted butterflies.

"You were meant for me," Bren had sung to him on their wedding night. A shabby room in a backstreet hotel, with a squeaky single bed and a rough grey wool blanket, had never been so romantic. Her beautiful voice sang out over the indigo sky filled with sparkling stars and an iridescent crescent moon.

Harry trudged back to the car, his normally upright shoulders drooping.

"Well?" said Susan.

His daughter had been persuaded to drive him over to the home to find out about the practicalities of cleaning up Brenda's belongings. What the protocols were. But Harry had forgotten to ask anything about them. The shock of the woman's words, that she had sat with his Bren, upset him. Why was it that she could, but he wasn't allowed to? He could feel the anger rising within him.

"I didn't ask," said Harry. "Take me home. Please."

"Dad, I've wasted a whole morning ..."

Harry put his hands up. "Stop it. Your mother asked very little of you, as have I. And now ... you can't give me a morning?" He shook his head.

"Sorry Dad, of course. I wasn't thinking. I'll go and ask as we are here, is that alright?"

"Thank you," he replied.

He looked at his daughter as she walked over to the front door. She was unlike her mother to look at, except in her walk. She had the same jaunty gait. Brenda had liked coordinating her wardrobe, Susan seemed to wear whatever came to hand, whether it matched or not. Certainly the plaid trousers she had on today argued with the patterned top. But she had inherited her mother's practical nature and he knew Susan would take no prisoners in the conversation with the staff. Just as she had done with the undertakers, organising what they were still permitted to arrange.

"I don't think I like this surreal new world," Harry muttered to himself.

"None of us do Dad," Susan said, climbing back into the car. "Sorted. Roger and I can go in on Sunday afternoon."

"Thank you. I wish I could take you for lunch somewhere," he said, looking at the closed shops and pubs and restaurants with their lights off, all with white notices in their windows.

"Soon Dad, we will be able to do things again."

Harry nodded. "I hope so." He was aware that he was living on borrowed time now. He had not seen anyone, other than through a window, for over three months. This trip with Susan did not feel like freedom. He had fought for it, but he now wondered what had been the point?"

As they turned into the driveway of the bungalow Harry noticed a wren sitting on the hedge. She was unusual for the area.

Sanitising his hands for the umpteenth time and slipping off the mask Susan had insisted on him wearing even in the car, Harry gave Susan a wave from the kitchen window as she reversed out of the drive. She had declined to stay for coffee in the garden.

"Just you and I then Jenny," Harry said to the tiny bird who had hopped onto a bush by the window.

It was a hot day, and Harry was tired. He walked around the block most days, despite the rules. He didn't want to lose the mobility he had, but he was too tired to do that today. He took his coffee and sandwich out to the garden.

The wren came closer, hopping from the bush onto the branch of the miniature apple tree Brenda planted when they first moved to the Bungalow. Jenny's tiny head bobbed up and down briefly as Harry studied her. He put out his hand. To his amazement, she hopped into his palm, and sat there, looking directly at him, with her head tilted.

Her brown feathers reminded him of Brenda's hair, before it turned silver.

"Well, you are well coordinated aren't you, little Jenny? Not like our Susan," Harry said softly, appreciating the cream and buff feathers of her underbelly. The long pink legs reminded him of ballet dancers' tights. The bird's head appeared to bob in agreement. She flew back onto the branch of the tree, watching him as he finished his lunch.

Brenda's legs were slim, he recalled. She had always regretted not being able to continue with ballet once the war started, but they had both enjoyed swing dancing and learning some of the more formal ballroom steps. Harry thought about the pale blue gown she had worn for the post wedding celebration her mother gave, she had never looked more beautiful, except for the day he had married her. They had both worn their uniforms. Brenda had carried a small bouquet of white blossom and lily of the valley hastily put together an hour before they were due to be married. He looked around the garden, the apple tree had already bloomed and the Lily of the Valley was also over. How much she had put into creating this beautiful oasis for them to enjoy. Sweet jasmine, fruit and vegetables, peonies and roses, the wild meadow at the bottom. Harry knew that his time was not yet up. Whatever else was going on in the world, as long as he had this space, he would always have his beloved Bren in his life. The way she had been, always would be in his mind and in his memory.

"Thank you, Jenny," he said to the bird as he cleared away his lunch.

And later, as he prepared for bed, and looked out at the crescent moon and twinkling stars he could see the silhouette of the little wren still sitting in the apple tree.

"Good night beautiful Bren," he said, humming *You Were Meant For Me*. He turned himself into bed, more content than he could remember, since Bren left.

"Sweet dreams, my love," he heard her say.

"Sweet dreams Bren," he replied.